LOVE'S PROMISE

Having worked the cruising circuit a number of years ago, Hannah now steps on board as a passenger, hoping for a relaxing break from her hectic life as a single parent. It's great to see some familiar faces and catch up with old friends. What she didn't bargain for was meeting her ex, and the father of her young son Charlie, on that ship! Then there's the bad-tempered Claudia, who won't leave him alone . . . Is Nick still that reckless adventurer, or could love really be lovelier the second time around?

JEAN ROBINSON

LOVE'S
PROMISE

Complete and Unabridged

LINFORD
Leicester

First published in Great Britain in 2019

First Linford Edition
published 2020

A catalogue record for this book is available
from the British Library.

ISBN 978–1–4448–4399–6

Published by
F. A. Thorpe (Publishing)
Anstey, Leicestershire

Set by Words & Graphics Ltd.
Anstey, Leicestershire
Printed and bound in Great Britain by
T. J. International Ltd., Padstow, Cornwall

This book is printed on acid-free paper

1

As soon as Hannah stepped on board the Bel Rosa she saw him and an involuntary gasp broke from her lips. She stopped breathing and her heart began to beat wildly. It couldn't be him. Not after all this time.

He stood, taller than she remembered, with an air of confidence he'd lacked all those years ago. The blond hair that had fallen over his forehead was shorter and darker now and neatly styled. He'd filled out a bit and his face had a healthy tan. He'd obviously moved up the ranks a scale or two by the braiding on his epaulettes, but there was no mistaking those blue-grey eyes and ready smile. She knew it was Nick.

His smile wasn't for her this time, though. Linking his arm was a glamorous blonde. Hannah wanted to run, hide, anything to escape the confusion his sudden appearance had thrown her into.

Then he caught her eye and the smile turned to a puzzled frown. He held her gaze for what seemed an age until eventually she managed to look away. Then, head down, she scurried towards the lifts. She could feel his eyes burrowing into her back — or maybe it was just her imagination. She wasn't going to look round to check. She had to get her head round the situation before she could face him — especially with this woman gazing up at him adoringly.

Stewards were guiding passengers to their accommodation but Hannah knew the layout of the ship. She'd sailed in one similar during her time as a hairdresser on board. That was when she'd first met Nick, one of the young chefs, five long years ago. It had been her first cruise, three weeks round the Greek islands. Nick had been on board for several months so knew the ropes. They'd fallen in love, but when the cruise ended, he'd gone home on leave and she'd been transferred to another ship — a Mediterranean cruise this time.

She hadn't seen or heard of him again. But she had never forgotten him . . . or forgiven him.

Once in the lift, she pressed the button for deck six where she knew her cabin was situated and then stood rigid trying to control her breathing. She'd been so looking forward to this cruise, had booked it months ago, a chance at last to visit these Mediterranean ports she'd only ever seen from the deck of a ship. But the shock of finding Nick on board had taken the excitement from her and renewed the pain she thought she had conquered long ago.

Trundling her hand luggage along the alleyway she found her cabin. Her case hadn't arrived yet but she hadn't expected it to be there with ten passenger decks for the porters to cover.

It was a nice little cabin with a bed set against one wall, a dressing table

3

beside it, and a rail for hanging clothes. From the small square window she could see a clear expanse of deck and, beyond it, the ship's rail.

After putting her hand luggage on the bed, she went exploring. Just along the alleyway from her cabin was a door leading out onto the deck. The sun was warm on her back as she leaned on the smooth wooden rail and looked down to the quay where the ship was moored.

Coaches were still arriving with passengers who were making their way towards the gangway. Beyond, she could just glimpse the huge statue of Christopher Columbus they'd passed in the coach that had brought her from the airport. It would have been nice to have spent some time in Barcelona instead of being transported straight to the ship. At least she would have a week there to explore at the end of the cruise before she flew home.

As she turned to go back inside she saw Nick striding along the deck heading in her direction.

He hesitated a moment as he stood awkwardly in front of her.

'Hannah, I can't believe it's you. What are you doing here?'

As their eyes met her heart began to thump and her legs turned to jelly.

'I've come on the cruise,' she mumbled, trying to keep her voice steady.

'What — you're a passenger?' He raised an enquiring eyebrow. 'Not hairdressing?'

'No, not this time. I'm a passenger.' It was on the tip of her tongue to tell him why, but he didn't deserve to know.

They stood staring at each other, unable to believe they had met up again.

Finally she managed to get her mind into gear and sound half normal. 'I see you stuck with it.'

'Yes, I'm still here,' he smiled, and her heart did a somersault. He let a brief pause fall. 'It's good to see you again, Hannah.'

Their conversation was rudely interrupted by a woman tugging at Nick's arm impatiently.

'We need bottled water in the salon,' the woman snapped. Hannah recognised her as the blonde she'd seen with Nick earlier.

Nick turned to her, visibly annoyed at the interruption. 'I'll send Sam down with some.'

'That boy is useless. I asked him yesterday to top the fridge up.'

'Give him a chance, Claudia. He only joined the ship two days ago.'

'That's no excuse. If he's not up to the job he shouldn't be on board. So what time are you finished tonight?'

Nick shrugged. 'When everything's sorted for next week.'

'You should delegate more,' Claudia grumbled with a swish of her long hair. She gave Hannah a questioning look as if she wondered who she was and why she was chatting to Nick, then flounced off. Nick shook his head as he watched her go.

Hannah looked away, not knowing how to respond to the interruption.

'Well, better get on,' he said, giving

her an apologetic smile.

She watched him saunter away, unable to believe what was happening. Finding Nick on board was bad enough. Knowing he was with this Claudia woman filled her with misgivings. The woman must be one of the catering staff.

Hannah's case was inside her room when she finally got back so she began to unpack and hang her dresses on the rail: the beautiful green evening dress she'd spent a whole week's wages on, the short blue one she'd bought because Josie had told her it matched her eyes. Remembering those shopping sprees with her sister made her smile despite the persistent knot that had formed inside her at seeing Nick.

It was all so long ago and over the years she'd learned to accept what had happened, but was never able to put it completely out of her mind. There was always a constant reminder in her little boy — the same kind eyes and the same cheeky smile. Other relationships had helped, but none had lasted. Now she was resigned to being on her own, and she was content. She had her sister and little Charlie, and it was enough.

At least, it had been until today when she'd seen him standing there, and the hurt felt as real as it had five years ago.

With everything neatly stowed away, Hannah went in search of the salon where she had once spent most of her days on cruises. She'd glimpsed one of the hairdressers on her way to her cabin and thought she recognised her. It would be nice if there was someone she knew on board.

As soon as she approached the salon she could smell the familiar scents. Her first glance inside took her back to her days working in a similar one on another ship, how tired she'd felt after being on her feet all day, and how lonely and homesick she'd been on that first cruise. Then she'd met Nick and everything had changed.

She straightened up, took a deep breath and walked inside. The room was pleasantly lit with plush red chairs set before gilt-rimmed mirrors. Immediately Hannah was back on that ship shampooing hair and dreaming of the evening when the salon would close and she could spend a few precious hours with Nick.

She heard voices and followed the sound into the treatment room beside the salon.

Then she stopped dead. Claudia stood talking to a young girl who was floating candles on a bowl of scented water. Hannah's heart sank. She hadn't anticipated this. She must be one of the beauticians.

'I'm afraid we're not open yet,' Claudia smilingly drawled when she saw Hannah there.

'I'm looking for Tess,' Hannah said. 'I just wanted to say hello.'

The smile faded. 'Tess hasn't appeared yet, and she'll be busy when she does get here. I should wait until tomorrow.'

Hannah hesitated. 'I'm Hannah. I used to work with Tess on cruise ships.'

Claudia looked decidedly unimpressed.

'Where do I put this, Claudia?' the young girl called out as she floated a flower head among the candles in the bowl.

Claudia turned to her in annoyance. 'I've told you already — on the table.'

'I'll give Tess your message,' she said dismissively to Hannah.

Hannah nodded and walked away, feeling the woman's eyes boring into her back — and immediately collided with Nick, nearly sending the huge box of fruit he was carrying flying.

He managed to steady it and gave her a bemused look. 'You're in a hurry to get somewhere.'

She apologised and smiled back. 'Sorry, I wasn't looking where I was going.'

'We'll have to stop meeting like this,' he quipped. 'Looking for anyone in particular?'

'I was trying to find out if Tess was on board,' she said as Nick hovered.

'Don't think I've met her.'

'We sailed together a few times. She's one of the hairdressers.'

'Ah, well, I don't come into contact with them very often.' His smile held a world of meaning but Hannah refused to respond. It did lighten the mood though, and she began to think it would be OK. If they could keep to this casual banter when they came into contact then she'd be able to cope. She didn't want a confrontation with him. It was all in the past — and that was where she wanted to leave it.

'It's all right for you to stand gossiping. I'd have thought you had more important things to do,' Claudia grumbled, coming through from the treatment room and giving Hannah a disapproving look. Hannah quickly averted her eyes.

'Everything's going smoothly,' Nick assured.

'Well, it might be in here too if everyone did their bit,' Claudia added with scorn.

'What's wrong?' he asked.

'Sam was supposed to bring that fruit down hours ago.'

'OK, but it's here now.'

She examined the box Nick was holding and pulled out an over-ripe peach. 'I can't put this out for clients. It's half rotten!'

'One peach,' Nick pointed out, plonking the box down on the reception desk.

'Not there,' Claudia snapped.

He closed his eyes and didn't reply, just picked it up again and followed her.

'You shouldn't be doing Sam's job for him,' Claudia said.

Nick let his breath out in a loud puff. 'Give him a chance. He's new, he'll learn.'

'And where's the bottled water?'

'That's on its way.'

Hannah grimaced and made her way out of the salon. She wasn't going to stand listening to any more of their bickering. At least now she knew Tess was on board.

Hunger was the last thing on her mind after all this trauma but she knew she would feel better if she ate. An early breakfast at the airport was all she'd had all day. The Terrace Buffet was her best bet. She'd get a light lunch there and eat it informally out on deck, alfresco style, and not feel as conspicuous as she would sitting alone in the formal restaurant.

The Terrace Buffet was light and airy, all big windows and bleached wood with an extensive buffet of hot and cold food along two walls. Sliding glass panels opened out onto a large expanse of deck where smartly dressed waiters moved between tables serving wine to people already seated, crisp white linen, silver cutlery and sparkling glassware dazzling in the brilliant sunshine.

Hannah joined the line of people at the buffet and decided the salad section looked most tempting.

'It's Hannah, isn't it?' A deep masculine voice came from behind her as she helped herself to a crusty bread roll. She turned and saw a stocky man with a jovial smile holding a plate containing a large slice of pizza.

It took a moment for recognition to dawn.

'Gary! It's you, Gary.'

'The very same.'

'Oh, it's so good to see you.' She almost dropped her plate of salad in an effort to give him a hug.

'So what are you doing down here at this time of day? Thought you'd be up to your eyes in shampoo.'

'No, I'm a passenger this time,' she said with a haughty toss of her head.

Gary looked surprised. 'Me, too. I'm with my mum. She always wanted to do a cruise but didn't fancy coming on her own so I'm chaperone.'

'Oh, that's lovely, Gary. I'll look forward to meeting her.'

'How about you? Not hairdressing any more?'

'Not on ships. I work in a salon back home now,' she replied.

'I gave up the cruises, too. There comes a time when you want to settle down.'

'So what are you up to now?'

'I'm working in a restaurant. It means I can keep an eye on Mum, too.'

They took their plates of food out on deck and found a table for two near the ship's rail where they would have a good view over the harbour. The water beneath them was calmly lapping the side of the ship as another huge cruise liner manoeuvred into the terminal. Rays of sunlight danced on the ripples making them sparkle. The sky was a cloudless azure blue.

'Where's your mum now?' Hannah asked, sliding into the chair the waiter had pulled out for her while Gary seated himself opposite and picked up the drinks menu.

'She wasn't hungry and said she'd wait till afternoon tea then indulge. She loves her cakes.'

Hannah laughed. 'Sensible lady!'

A waiter came to ask what they'd like to drink.

'I fancy a beer,' Gary said, looking to Hannah.

'White wine for me, please.'

Conversation buzzed around them as Gary chattered on about his life since leaving the cruise ships and how he'd managed to buy a house near to his mum. They talked of old times on ships they'd been on, and by the time they'd finished their meal Hannah felt much better. Finding Gary on board had given a huge boost to her confidence.

'Well, better see what Mum's up to,' Gary said eventually, getting up from the table. 'Maybe we can meet up later?'

'That would be lovely,' Hannah said, scribbling her cabin number on a serviette and handing it to him.

She decided not to go straight back to her cabin but to take a wander round the ship. The promenade deck would be a good place to start. Some exercise and fresh air was needed after the journey here.

The sun was hot as she walked, smiling at others who seemed to be doing the same. The cruise terminal where the ship was moored was so near the waterside promenade she could see passengers were still pouring up the gangway. Soon they would all be on board and the ship would set sail.

After several circuits, she dropped down to the pool deck where those already on board were gathering, chatting in groups. Several had found loungers and were already soaking up the late June sunshine. Potted palms round the pool wafted gently in the breeze. Above them, the upper decks, mounted one upon the other, dazzled white in the sunshine.

She wasn't a sun worshipper so made her way inside to explore the rest of the ship deck by deck. There were several bars and a variety of restaurants, shops, a library and a cinema. People were milling around looking at all the places on board, just as she was.

The Skylight Bar was a huge space high up in the ship with low, round tables and grey velvet sofas set before huge picture windows giving views across the harbour and out towards the sea. The central bar with its blue padded stools would not open until the ship sailed.

Hannah had occasionally managed a drink with Nick at a bar like this late in the evening when his duties in the galley had finished. Sometimes they had gone to the nightclub to listen to a group playing and then danced until the early hours. She hadn't slept much during those three weeks. Life had become too exciting. Then all too quickly it had ended.

She shook herself back to the present, determined not to let intrusive thoughts consume her. The room was quiet now, with only a few people relaxing near the windows reading newspapers or dozing. She wandered round taking in the view from every window, then settled herself on one of the sofas and stared out across the harbour and let it sooth her troubled mind.

She must have dozed off, for when she woke she saw Nick behind the bar checking bottles of spirit and for a moment thought she was back on that first cruise waiting for him to finish so that they could spend some time together.

Then reality dawned.

He had his back to her and she wondered if she could sneak out unseen. But he turned and gave her one of his charming smiles as she approached the entrance.

'I'm checking everything's in order before we open up. Sam, our new barman, is not very experienced.'

'Claudia didn't seem too impressed with him,' Hannah remarked, as some comment was obviously called for.

'It takes a lot to impress Claudia. Which reminds me, I haven't sent that water to her yet.'

'You'll be in trouble,' she retorted.

'I'm always in trouble,' he said without smiling this time and continued with his task.

Hannah turned to leave as Nick twisted back to face her, a look of concern clouding his face. 'Don't let Claudia bother you,' he said.

'I won't, but she was very abrupt with me when I asked about Tess. Is she always that rude?'

'I'm afraid so.'

'Well, I shall try to avoid her.'

'She gets stressed when a new lot of passengers come on board.'

Nick paused and gave her a penetrating glance. 'We're not together, you know. I only met her a couple of voyages ago when I joined this ship.'

'Well, that's really none of my business,' Hannah said emphatically.

'No, but I didn't want you to get the wrong impression.'

'I haven't formed any impression. I'm just surprised you take it from her.' She felt her jaw stiffen but managed to keep her voice calm.

'It makes for a peaceful life and she's OK when she's in a good mood.'

'Well, I'm off to finish unpacking now.'

'Don't forget boat drill in half an hour,' he said, in a lighter tone of voice.

'How could I, with the emergency alarm blasting out all over the ship?'

Their conversation played on Hannah's mind as she wandered back to her cabin.

Why had Nick been so intent on telling her that he and Claudia were not together? Claudia had asked him what time he would be finished. Presumably that meant they would be getting together then. Trying to shrug off these unwanted thoughts, she continued to pound the deck for another three circuits.

★   ★   ★

Although she was expecting it, the emergency alarm for the mandatory boat drill did startle her. She pulled the lifejacket from its shelf, strapped it on and hurried along the alleyways towards the exit that would take her to the muster station.

The first person she set eyes on was Claudia. There she was, standing alongside the lifeboat. But Nick wasn't beside her. Then she saw him busily helping one of the passengers who was still struggling with the straps of his lifejacket. She watched as he chatted with the elderly gentleman then he straightened and scanned the deck and spotted her.

Hannah watched as Claudia moved to stand beside him. There appeared to be sharp words from Claudia but Nick seemed oblivious to her presence. Claudia followed his line of gaze and looked directly at Hannah, suspicion written all over her face. She turned back to Nick and snapped out a few more words then stalked off.

Hannah quickly looked away. Thankfully her attention was taken by a young officer asking her name. He gave a friendly smile, ticked her off his list and moved on. It lessened the tension a little. Then the small lady who'd been standing beside her introduced herself as Nancy. They began to chat about the drill and what a fuss it all was. Hannah was glad of the distraction and tried to explain to her how important it was for safety.

'But a ship like this isn't going to sink, is it?' Nancy said with a grin.

Hannah reassured her that was unlikely. 'But if there was a fire we may have to abandon ship.'

'I hope that doesn't happen,' Nancy said, with a twinkle in her eye.

'Don't worry, it won't take long then you can go and have a nice cup of tea,' Hannah told her and was rewarded with a warm smile.

When Nancy moved away Hannah cast her eyes towards where Nick and Claudia had been standing and breathed a sigh of relief when there was no sign of either of them.

Once back in her cabin she looked along the row of dresses she'd bought for the cruise, determined to put Nick and Claudia out of her mind. She had no idea what she would do during the evening. Gary had suggested they meet up at some point, and knowing how people dressed up on cruises, she wanted to look her best. She would glam up just like everyone else and go out there and enjoy whatever presented itself. There was usually a good show on at the theatre and later in the evening the nightclub would spring to life with live music and dancing. She was not going to let this business with Nick ruin her holiday.

Just as she was about to change there was a gentle tap at her door. She tensed, fearing it might be Nick or Claudia, then breathed a sigh of relief when she found Gary standing outside.

'I wandered if you'd like to come down to the sail-away cocktail party out on deck with me.'

Feeling happier, she smiled up at him. 'That would be lovely. I'd forgotten all about it.'

'I'll meet you on the pool deck in an hour's time. Then after the party we can go and eat.'

She showered and changed, humming happily to herself. Before leaving the room she glanced at her reflection in the mirror and was satisfied she looked her best: fair curly hair brushed into submission, a slight blush to her pale cheeks and a pretty floral summer dress that fitted her slim figure to perfection. She slung her bag over her shoulder and skipped happily down the alleyway and out onto the deck.

2

The sail-away party was in full swing, the ship now gliding through still water, making its way round the peninsula. Astern of them the waterfront of Barcelona with its impressive buildings was set in sharp relief against the pale blue of a twilight sky.

As soon as Hannah appeared on deck Gary was at her side. Together they stood at the edge of the gathering and took in the scene. Pale pink lanterns hung over the large expanse of wooden deck, their pale glow reflecting in the still water of the swimming pool. In the early evening light it looked quite magical.

A Brazilian band beside the pool played lively music as people stood chatting, calling to friends or just standing at the rail staring down at the churning water as the ship ploughed its steady course out towards the open sea.

A waiter approached with a silver tray of cocktails held high in one hand. Gary took one of the tall frosted glasses topped with fruit and straws and tiny umbrellas and gave it to Hannah, then took one for himself. Slowly they merged into the crowd and stood absorbing the atmosphere.

'You look lovely,' Gary said.

Hannah felt herself blush but the compliment boosted her confidence. She was glad Josie had persuaded her to buy the flowery dress she was wearing. The colours in it suited her fair complexion and the simple style with the halter neck was cool and comfortable for a warm summer evening.

'Is your mum not coming?' Hannah asked.

'She's already here. Can't keep Mum away from a party.' He scanned the deck. 'There she is, gossiping with that couple.'

Hannah looked to where he was pointing. 'Do you mean the lady in blue?'

'That's my mum. You'll meet her later.'

Hannah grinned at him. 'I already

have. We were chatting together at the lifeboat drill. She didn't seem to think much of it.'

'Oh, I know all about that!'

'I didn't see you there.'

He gave her a roguish smile. 'I was hiding behind the lifeboat. She embarrasses me sometimes.'

'Oh, but she's lovely,' Hannah said.

They fell into comfortable silence watching the land slipping by, feeling the gentle rhythm of the sea as the sun settled low towards the horizon turning the sky a blaze of colour and burnishing the ship's white paintwork with a golden glow.

Gary pointed to the shoreline with its long stretches of golden beach. 'Look, you can see the waterside promenade. It's beautiful along there with all the big hotels. And there's the marina — there's lots of bars and restaurants around it, a good place to spend an evening.'

Hannah felt a bubble of excitement rising inside her. 'I'm staying on there for a week after the cruise so I'll be able to go exploring.'

A breeze blew up and Hannah had to hold her dress down. 'I don't think you can have a hair style on board a ship,' she said, as her carefully arranged curls blew round her face.

With the party atmosphere on board, she had almost forgotten about Nick. When Gary disappeared to get another drink for them, she scanned the deck. There was no sign him, but it was difficult to see with so many people crowded together. Anyway, he would be busy. The crew never got time for socialising so she should be safe from any encounters for this evening at least.

Some couples were dancing in front of the musicians as others watched and swayed to the music. Flags fluttered from the masts. The atmosphere was charged with excited anticipation. Eventually, however, the crowd on deck began to thin as people went in for dinner.

'I'd better rescue Mum now. She keeps looking at me,' Gary said.

'Does she need rescuing? I'd have

thought she was well able to look after herself.'

'Not from that couple. Or rather, that man. I met him earlier. He's called Bryn and full of his own importance. He'd bore the socks off you if you let him. His poor wife never gets a word in edgeways. I think he's found a good listener in Mum. She wouldn't dare walk away.'

'OK, let's prise her free, then,' Hannah said, giving him a cheeky glance.

Nancy looked more than relieved when she saw them approaching. 'This is my son,' she told Bryn with pride.

The portly gentleman with red face and curled moustache looked Gary up and down then extended a large hand.

'Just been putting your mum in the picture,' Bryn barked. 'Need to know your way round on these cruises.'

'Gary used to be a waiter on board,' Nancy informed him. 'He knows his way round.'

'Hmm.' Bryn took his wife's arm.

'Come along, my dear. We don't want be late for dinner.'

They watched as the elderly couple trundled off and disappeared through one of the heavy doors.

'What a bore,' Nancy said. 'I feel sorry for his wife.' Then she caught Hannah's eye and they both suppressed a snort of laughter.

'We thought you were enjoying his company,' Hannah said, teasing.

Nancy gave her a conspiratorial look. 'You wicked girl!'

'Come on then, ladies,' Gary said, taking one on each arm. 'Let me escort you to dinner.'

'Shall we eat out on the terrace tonight?' Nancy suggested. 'It's such a lovely evening. It would be a shame to sit indoors in the main restaurant.'

'Anything to please a lady,' Gary said, chivalrous as ever. He turned to Hannah. 'Is that all right with you? I think they have waiter service in the evening.'

'Yes, I'd like that.'

The Terrace Restaurant was busy but Gary managed to find them a table out on deck. The ship was on the open sea now but the air was still warm. As dusk closed in, lights on board shed a cosy glow. Hannah glanced at Gary across the table and he gave her a warm smile. She returned it, feeling happy and comfortable.

After dinner Nancy said she would retire for the night. Gary looked towards Hannah.

'There's a group playing in the Hub later. Never heard of them but they may be good. Fancy it?'

Hannah hesitated. She didn't want to appear unsociable but felt emotionally drained.

'It doesn't usually get going until late,' she said.

'You're right. It *has* been a tiring day. Perhaps an early night is called for,' Gary agreed.

Hannah nodded gratefully.

'I'll sit out here on deck for a while, then make for bed.'

'And I'll go and check on Mum,' he said, smiling. 'See you in the morning.'

She wandered towards the ship's side and stared out at the rose-washed evening sea with a feeling of contentment. She'd enjoyed being with Gary and his mum but now wanted time to herself to calmly assimilate the events of the day, the shock of finding Nick on board and the emotions it had reignited when she'd thought she had put it all behind her.

Alongside her, the pool deck bar was busy serving drinks. A few couples were sitting quietly chatting and enjoying the late evening air. The sound of bow waves skimming the sides of the ship mingled with the friendly banter of a small group further along. Lights from above the bar gave a warm glow. Hannah leant on the ship's rail staring out across the ocean, lulled by the rhythm of the ship as it ploughed its way through the Mediterranean Sea towards St Tropez, their first port of call.

Now, after a long day, she was ready

for bed. On passing a sign to the Hub on her way to her cabin she decided to poke her nose in and see what sort of group were playing.

With a slight feeling of trepidation she ventured inside and stood by the entrance surveying the scene. The night-club was buried deep within the ship, its mirrored walls giving the impression of space. Yet the subtle lighting in secluded alcoves created an intimate cosy feel.

It was crowded and noisy. Blue strobe lighting flashed across a stage where a group of musicians belted out heavy metal. A few people were gyrating on a small patch of dance floor in front of the stage, but most were crowded round the bar at the far end.

She stood watching from the edge and was just about to leave when she spotted Claudia on the small square of dance floor. She wore very tight jeans and a designer top. Her silky blonde hair fell straight around her shoulders, and she was giving it her all.

When the music changed to a slower

pace most people left the floor, but Claudia moved into the arms of a very tall man and draped herself around him. It wasn't Nick.

Hannah searched the room for Nick but there was no sign of him. She looked towards the bar at the far end but the lighting had dimmed and she couldn't see clearly.

On her way back to her cabin, she was drawn to the sound of gentle night music drifting in from somewhere out on deck. Slipping through the first door she could find, she followed the sound. Looking down over the rail to the deck below she could see a small group of musicians entertaining passengers sitting by one of the deck bars. A soft voiced woman began to croon a love song, one that always brought a lump to her throat.

Almost immediately she became aware of someone moving to stand behind her and turned to see Nick, his face shadowy in the moonlight.

'Memories,' he whispered as he moved

beside her at the rail.

Just hearing his soft, deep voice sent a ripple of desire coursing through her. After a few moments silence he turned and she was forced to look at him. He wore a fresh open-necked shirt and she could just detect the musky hint of cologne.

'We danced to this one,' he murmured.

'Under a harvest moon,' she breathed.

'It's been a long time, Hannah.'

'Five years.'

There was a long pause as they watched the musicians on the deck below. Then he moved closer and a shiver ran down her spine as their bare arms touched.

'I've often thought about you,' he said, unaware of the turmoil his closeness was stirring.

'Why didn't you keep in touch?'

'I don't know.'

She turned away from him, unable to bear the sadness in his smile.

'I was afraid to. I didn't see how it could work. Both of us away on different ships.'

'You could have talked to me about it,' she managed in a shaky voice.

'I know. I'm sorry.'

They stood in silence for some moments. Then she sensed him move away. She stood quite still staring out into the darkness, her whole body wracked with longing, until she was able to make her legs carry her back to her cabin.

With a feeling of relief, she fell onto the bed and let the tears flow as memories consumed her. He'd told her he loved her on their last evening together, that soon they would be together again. But after he had left the ship there had been nothing. No response to her phone calls. No reply to her emails. Nothing. If only he'd talked to her and explained his fears, it might all have worked out differently.

Despondently she undressed and climbed into bed. Almost immediately exhaustion kicked in and sleep took all her pain away.

★ ★ ★

The following morning Hannah woke to a beautiful coral sky, a mist still lingering over the ocean. She dressed in shorts and sun top and fastened her wayward curls into a ponytail to keep them out of the way. Holding her head high, she walked confidently into the Terrace Buffet in search of breakfast.

People were beginning to fill the tables out on deck. Some had chosen to sit inside but most wanted to enjoy the lovely weather and the approaches to St Tropez. Hannah took her plate of food outside and found a small table by the rail. The sea was calm with only the movement of the ship disturbing its surface, the sky now a clear blue with not a cloud in sight. Further along the deck, a woman stood taking photos. Waiters moved smoothly between the tables serving coffee and juices. She lifted her face to enjoy the warmth of the early morning sun.

A tall, big-boned woman with short bobbed hair stood looking for a table. The lady caught Hannah's eye and, seeing she was sitting alone, headed towards her.

'Would you mind if I joined you?' she asked in a rather posh voice as she stood looking down at Hannah, tall and straight in white trousers and a striped blue shirt.

Hannah wasn't keen. She was enjoying the solitude of the beautiful morning but felt she couldn't be rude so indicated the empty chair opposite with a forced smile.

The lady put her plate on the table then sat with a rigid back looking down at her thin slices of Parma ham and two crusty rolls.

'Wouldn't contemplate eating this at home for breakfast,' she said at last.

Hannah smiled. 'No, but it's good to have a change when you're on holiday.'

'Oh, absolutely,' the lady replied, her expression lightening. 'I'm Linda, by the way.'

As they introduced themselves a waiter took their coffee order.

'Are you traveling alone?' Linda asked Hannah.

'Yes, I'm afraid so.'

Linda shook her head vigorously. 'No, no, you mustn't think like that. We women are quite capable of looking after ourselves. I enjoy my independence, wouldn't want to be tied down with a husband.'

'Chance would be a fine thing,' Hannah said.

Linda gave her an incredulous look.

'You'd like to have one?'

'No, I'm quite content on my own.' She wasn't about to open her heart to a complete stranger.

'I should think so. I can't imagine living with the same man for years on end,' Linda continued.

'No,' Hannah said without conviction.

The conversation drifted on to how lovely the ship was and their expectation of the places they were to visit. Hannah was surprised at how easily the conversation flowed. When they were done Linda got up and left with just a polite comment on how she had enjoyed Hannah's company.

Next, Hannah wanted to see Tess.

Though reluctant to go back to the salon for fear of coming up against Claudia again, she was determined not to let it stop her.

'Hannah!' Tess shrieked as soon as she saw her. She plonked the towels she was carrying down on the reception desk and the two women hugged each other.

'Come on in,' Tess said, leading her into the salon. 'What are you doing here?'

'Don't worry, I'm not about to relieve you of your job,' Hannah joked. 'I'm doing the cruise.'

'You mean you're a passenger?'

'That's right. So you'd better be nice to me.'

Tess pulled out a chair from one of the mirrors so Hannah could sit while she busied herself tidying the shelf. 'It's really good to see you. I often wondered what had happened to you.'

'I gave up the cruises eventually.'

'So what are you doing now? Still hairdressing?' Tess said, as she ran a polishing cloth over the mirror in front of her.

'I work for my sister as a stylist in her salon.'

'Still in Leicester?'

'Yes, Josie lets me live in the flat above which is very convenient.'

'Not married, then?' Tess asked.

'No, how about you?'

'No, never met the right man. Don't suppose I ever will now. Think I'm too set in my ways. It's hard to sustain a relationship in this job.'

There weren't any clients in the salon yet but Hannah knew it wouldn't be long before the first ones began to arrive for their appointments.

'Look, we'll have a proper catch up later when I get a break,' Tess said, glancing to the entrance.

Hannah got up. 'Yes, that would be great,'

'I expect you're off to St Tropez when the ship moors,' Tess said as they walked to the desk.

'That's the plan.'

'How's your French?' Tess asked as she checked the screen for her first appointment.

'Only what I can remember from school.'

Tess turned from the screen and began to adjust the floral arrangement on the reception desk. 'Well, you enjoy yourself. I wish I could come with you but I've got bookings all day.'

'I thought everyone would be ashore,' Hannah said. 'St Tropez is supposed to be the most famous resort on the Riviera. All those luxury yachts in the harbour and villas on the peninsula. I remember how the passengers used to rave about it when they came back on board.'

'I know, I've heard it all too. It certainly has one of the most beautiful bays with cafés and shops all around the harbour. But that's all I've seen of it. And that was from the deck of the ship. Always wanted to go ashore there myself.'

'Well, it's taken me long enough.'

'At least you're doing it. After ten years I'm still slogging away in here.' She sighed, then shrugged. 'I wouldn't want it otherwise, though. Can't imagine doing anything else now.'

'Gary's asked me if I'd like to go ashore with him this afternoon,' Hannah told her.

Tess looked at her. 'You work fast. Only been on board a few hours and you've already found yourself a man!'

'You know Gary. He used to wait on table. He's here as a passenger with his mum.'

'Of course I remember Gary. I've sailed with him several times. Always cheerful, never causes any trouble.'

'He said he was going for a look round and would I like to join him.'

'Gary's a great guy. You go off and make the best of it while you can,' Tess said.

'I'm grateful for the offer. I would have been nervous going on my own in case I got lost and didn't get back on time.'

'Needn't worry about that with Gary. He knows his way round. You'll be quite safe with him.'

Tess glanced round the salon to make sure everything was in order and Hannah thought how lovely it looked. She'd forgotten the trouble they went to so that their clients would experience the height of luxury and pampering. Soft music played in the background and a soothing aroma emanated from the treatment room.

When Hannah peeked through the connecting screen Tess noticed and chuckled.

'You won't find Madam in yet. She never appears until at least ten o'clock. Too fond of her bed, she is.'

'Do you mean Claudia?'

'Who else?' Tess laughed.

Well, I know who she'll be with, Hannah thought as a sharp pang of jealousy stabbed through her. But she kept her feelings to herself.

When Nancy walked through the door, Hannah felt her spirits lift again.

'I thought I'd get in before the rush,' Nancy said, giving her a warm smile.

Tess began to guide Nancy towards

the wash basin and Hannah prepared to leave.

'Don't leave on my behalf, dear,' Nancy said. 'You two carry on chatting. I love a bit of gossip.'

Hannah followed them to the wash-basin, while Tess draped a towel round Nancy's shoulders. She didn't feel she should disappear when Nancy had indicated that she would like her to stay. A bit of cheerful gossip was what she needed.

'Just a nice head massage and then set it in rollers, will you, dear?' Nancy told Tess. 'I can't be doing with these blow-dries. I've had a perm, so what's the point in straightening it all out?'

'It won't straighten it,' Tess explained. 'I could blow dry it into a gentle wave. Why don't you try it? If you don't like it, I'll put some rollers in.'

Nancy looked doubtful, then she smiled her lovely smile.

'Why not?' Then she chortled. 'Eh, my Gary'll think I'm getting above meself with fancy hairdos.'

Hannah couldn't help laughing at her words.

'You'll be the belle of the ball when Tess has finished with you,' she assured her.

Nancy leaned back and let Tess massage the shampoo into her hair while they kept up their chat and Hannah was glad of the distraction as she began to feel her nerves relax.

Claudia did eventually show up, looking bleary-eyed and hung over. She disappeared into the treatment room without not so much as a nod to them. Tess looked at Hannah and they both stifled a chuckle.

Nancy was thrilled with her new hairstyle and booked another appointment for later in the week.

'I want to look nice this evening,' she told Hannah. 'I was too tired to bother last night. But I'll keep my hair like this now. It makes me look younger, don't you think?'

'I think it looks very nice,' Hannah told her.

And it did. Nancy had such a lovely, happy face that she would have looked good whatever hair style she'd settled on.

Once Nancy left, Tess tidied the area and then turned to Hannah. 'Fancy a coffee, say in an hour's time? I'm booked solid after that.'

'Sounds good,' Hannah said, glancing at her watch. 'Just time for a swim.'

3

The swimming pool out on deck was remarkably quiet as Hannah approached. A few people were sunbathing on the loungers set round its edge. There was only one swimmer gliding up and down the pool's length. Hannah stood watching, admiring his powerful stroke — then realised it was Nick.

He reached the end and pulled himself out of the water where he sat breathing deeply. When he saw her he smiled, got up and began to walk round the pool to where she was standing, his well-toned body glistening with water droplets.

She was tempted to pretend she hadn't seen him and walk away, but he had already caught her eye so she felt obliged to stay put.

'Shirking your duties,' she said, determined to keep the conversation casual.

'I've been up since dawn, unlike some people,' he said, obviously happy to be back to the light-hearted banter.

'Well, as a passenger, I do have the privilege of a leisurely breakfast,' she mocked.

'OK, don't rub it in. Are you off ashore in St Tropez later?'

'Yes, I'm going with Gary.'

There was a tiny shift in his expression.

'You mean Gary who used to be a waiter?'

'Yes.'

'Didn't know he was on board.'

'Yes, we're both passengers this time.'

His mood changed suddenly and he hunched his shoulders. 'Well, have a good day, then.'

Hannah frowned as he strode away purposefully. What had got into him? Just when it seemed they had got over the shock of seeing each other again and were trying to be civilised. Ah, well, there was no telling with Nick. As unpredictable as ever.

49

She slipped into the pool and began to swim up and down to try to put the whole incident out of her mind, and soon felt calmer again.

★ ★ ★

The coffee bar was situated in a large, open space at the centre of the ship, together with designer shops and a long, busy information desk. Shelves of books separated the various areas, with tall lamps illuminating cosy corners. Soft music played in the background as passengers sat reading newspapers or chatting quietly near the surrounding windows, the atmosphere calm and relaxed.

Tess and Hannah collected their coffee, then sat at one of the window tables. No sooner were they seated when Tess sighed and, following her gaze, Hannah saw Claudia standing surveying the room.

'Don't look, then maybe she won't see us,' Tess said.

But Claudia was heading directly towards their table. She pulled out a seat and plonked herself heavily down on it.

'You're taking an early break, aren't you?' Tess said. 'You've only just got up.'

Claudia ignored the dig and yawned. 'No bookings 'till eleven.'

Hannah suppressed a snort.

'I can't wait to get out of this business and settle down,' Claudia sighed.

'So where is lover-boy?' Tess asked.

'That man is driving me crazy. I can't get him out of the galley. I don't know what's got into him all of a sudden.'

'Doesn't sound like Nick to me. I thought he was happy to delegate. He's usually in the bar every evening and then down in the Hub until late when it closes.'

'Exactly. Well, I've told him straight. I'm not putting up with it.'

'You'd better be careful. Nick's not the type to take threats.'

Claudia gave her a wry smile. 'Oh, I can get round Nick all right, don't you worry.'

Tess gave Hannah an amused look. But Hannah couldn't think of a thing to say. So much for Nick saying that he and Claudia weren't together. It sounded as if they were very much together if Claudia was planning on settling down with him.

She did not want this conversation with this woman so she quickly made her excuses and left them at the table. Tess gave her a questioning look but Hannah ignored it. Claudia just glared after her as if she didn't know who she was or why she'd been sitting with Tess.

Once out on deck, Hannah breathed deeply to calm herself. She really had to get a grip. Her behaviour was unacceptable. Tess was probably wondering right now what was wrong with her.

When she felt her legs would carry her, she walked purposefully towards the stern of the ship until she found a quiet area of deck where she could be alone with her thoughts.

A stab of ferocious anger caught her unawares. Again she had fallen into the same trap, believing what Nick told her, when she should have realised by now that he couldn't be trusted. Claudia was most definitely his girlfriend and they had obviously talked about settling down together.

Leaning on the rail, she stared mesmerised at the trail of seafoam the ship created as it glided through the still blue water and slowly her heartbeat steadied until after a while she felt she could let it go. Shading her eyes, she stared out over the sea. She loved the tangy smell of it, the shifting colours, blues and purples mixed with grey. She had Josie and Charlie. Thinking about her sister and her little boy brought a warm glow of happiness.

The ship was cruising towards the bay of St Tropez. A distant yacht tacked into the wind, its sails billowing. High on its rocky promontory, the citadel came into view, then after passing the old fortifications, Hannah got a glimpse of the picturesque harbour and remembered how excited she had been when she'd first seen it.

Knowing the ship would soon be

anchoring offshore, she wandered back to her cabin, checked her bag for all the essentials: sun cream, sun glasses, hat. Keeping her fair skin protected was a must. She couldn't afford to expose it to these Mediterranean rays or she'd end up looking like a beetroot — not a look she wished to adopt!

As soon as they were moored, she took the lift to the lower deck where the gangway would connect to the tender that would take them ashore. Several people were gathered and soon began to move through security and onto the small boat. Gary was waiting for her at the top of the gangway and greeted her with his usual cheerful smile, taking her hand to help her onto the tender.

Everyone clambered on board the small boat, happy people chatting and laughing, all squashed up on long bench seats that ran the length of its deck. Gary was his usual jovial self and joined in the banter. Finally Hannah was able to put Nick to the back of her mind as the holiday mood took over.

Just as the boatman was releasing the ropes to pull away, Nick jumped on board and her whole body tensed. She watched as he spoke a few words with the boatman and surveyed the passengers sitting under the awning. She quickly looked away but Gary recognised him at once.

'Hey, what are you doing here, old man?' Gary called out.

'Same as you, mate,' Nick called back, looking relaxed as ever. 'Taking the chance to get off the ship while I can. Always been my favourite port in the Med, this one.'

As the two men chatted, Hannah tried to control her emotions.

Nick settled himself on the edge of the boat and took up a conversation with the boatman.

'Fancy Nick being on the ship. I haven't seen him in years. We sailed together a few times,' Gary said, turning to Hannah.

Hannah tried to make sensible comments but her mind was in turmoil. If Nick joined them for the afternoon she knew she would not be able to relax and enjoy her time ashore.

It was only minutes before they reached the quay with all its bustling life. Pavement cafés along the waterfront were busy as people sat enjoying cool drinks while admiring the huge yachts moored in the bay. Many small shops were set amid quaint stone buildings, all glowing golden in the afternoon sunshine.

Nick jumped off the boat and helped to tie it up alongside, then stood helping the passengers alight onto the quay. As Hannah stepped off he took her hand to steady her and their eyes met. He held onto her a moment longer than was necessary and his touch set all her nerves tingling. It took her totally unawares and she quickly looked away, embarrassed.

Once safely ashore, Gary was at her side.

'I don't know where Nick's disappeared to. I thought he might join us but there's no sign of him now.'

As they began to walk along the promenade and merge with the crowd Hannah found it difficult not to look round to see if Nick was following them.

'A lot of famous artists painted here,' Gary was telling her as they stood for a while watching one at work at his easel.

'Looks as if they still do,' Hannah said, desperately trying to keep her mind on what he was saying.

'It's hard to believe it was once a small fishing village,' Gary said, glancing around him as yachts manoeuvred in and out of their moorings, some setting sail for the open sea, others securing their boats with ropes as they prepared for a day ashore.

While they watched the scene unfolding before them Hannah forced herself to calm down.

'So, how did it become home to the rich and famous?' she managed to ask Gary.

'I think Brigitte Bardot had a lot to do with that. You get to see her mansion if you do the boat trip round the harbour.' They exchanged glances. 'Do you fancy that?' he suggested.

'Yes — let's see how the other half live.'

'It's quite eye-popping to see the mansions and yachts close up. I did it once. Managed to get an afternoon off the ship.'

They boarded a boat that was just leaving and tucked themselves into the shade of the wheelhouse out of the burning sun. More people piled on until it became crowded, then it pulled away from the landing stage and was off at speed into Millionaire's Bay.

Sitting close together on the bench seat and leaning back on the wood of the wheelhouse, Hannah finally felt herself relax. At least she knew Nick wasn't on this boat.

Soon she was on the edge of her seat staring in awe at the mansions scattered along the coast of the peninsula and high up among its rocky crags. The captain gave a running commentary on the rich and famous people they belonged to with some amusing details that had them all laughing.

'I don't know if I'd want one of those,' Gary said. 'Seems a bit cut off to me.'

'I'd rather be in the town where all the life is,' Hannah agreed.

They stared up at a yacht floating gently past.

'I can only see two people. Look, they're sitting up on the top deck,' Hannah exclaimed.

'The crew will be down below doing all the work,' Gary said with feeling.

'Fancy having a crew all to yourself! I feel spoiled just being on a ship like ours and being waited on.'

'That's what Mum said yesterday. I don't think she's ever been waited on in her life. It's why I came with her. She's always wanted to do a cruise but I knew she wouldn't come on her own.'

'She's a lovely lady, your mum,' Hannah said.

'Yes, she is, and she likes you. She said how nice you and Tess had been when she had her hair done and how you'd persuaded her to have it in a different style.'

Hannah smiled. 'It wasn't so very different but it pleased her and that's all that matters.'

They sat back in their seats as the boat suddenly veered away from the land and towards the middle of the harbour. Rays of sunlight danced on the ripples making the water sparkle. Beneath the clear blue sky Hannah felt a wonderful contentment settle on her.

Then she was on her feet again. 'There's our ship,' she gasped, trying to get a better view through all the cameras held high by other passengers in an effort to get a photo of the Bel Rosa at anchor just at the edge of the bay. It sat there, majestically towering above the small boat and glowing golden in the afternoon sunshine.

Hannah stood mesmerised, remembering how she'd felt when she'd set eyes on her very first cruise ship, how impressed she had been, yet intimidated too. A young hairdresser, first time away from home, she'd been lonely and homesick. Until she'd met Nick.

'Quite a spectacle, isn't it?' Gary said, breaking into her thoughts.

'Yes,' she said. A lump had formed in her throat making it difficult for her to speak.

Gary noticed and put a comforting arm round her shoulders as they continued to stare up at the huge white side of the ship.

'Memories?' he whispered.

'Yes,' she murmured, although Gary wouldn't know what those memories were. He would just think she was being sentimental. She blinked hard to stop tears that threatened to overflow.

Gary steered her back to her seat and sat quietly beside her. As the small boat turned and aimed back towards the quay she managed to regain her composure.

Back on dry land they wandered up from the seafront promenade into a maze of narrow streets and ambled along absorbing the colour and atmosphere of the charming town with its tiny boutiques, galleries and antique shops.

'We have to try the Tropezienne Tart,'

Hannah announced as they viewed the pavement cafés, busy with people enjoying refreshments.

Gary gave her a puzzled look. 'Do we?'

Hannah laughed, her spirit restored amid the throng of holiday makers and the warm sunshine. It was difficult to be sad in Gary's company.

They settled for a small patisserie and sat at a table under a brightly coloured sun umbrella. A waiter was instantly with them, took their order and was soon back with their tea and pastries.

'It is rather good,' Gary agreed as he sank his teeth into the cream-filled tart.

When they returned to the waterfront they agreed there was just time for a glass of wine before the tender was due to take them back to the ship. It wasn't difficult to find a bar as there were so many around the bustling harbour.

'It's funny seeing Nick again after so long,' Gary said. 'I wonder where he was off to? He disappeared rather quickly.'

'I expect he was making for the nearest bar. He probably knows people here if it's his favourite port,' Hannah said, trying to keep her voice steady and casual.

Gary nodded. 'Guess so. He'll have done all the touristy things. We kept in touch for a while. He always had a girlfriend in tow but they never lasted — a free spirit, is Nick. Never wanted to be tied down.'

As they chatted on Hannah began to see more clearly what had happened. All these girlfriends . . . she had just been one of them. It seemed Claudia was just another he had now tired of. A free spirit, Gary said. If only she had worked that out sooner, she could have spared herself so much heartache.

They finished their drinks and walked back to the quay. Nick was last to board, jumping on as they were almost away. He sat up with the boatman again. Gary joined him and they chatted for a while. When Gary came back to sit beside Hannah he looked puzzled.

'He doesn't seem to remember me,' he said. 'Acted very strangely, in fact, not like Nick at all. He used to be a friendly guy.'

Hannah looked away. She couldn't bring herself to get into another conversation about Nick.

Once back on board the Bel Rosa, Gary said he would go and check on his mum and Hannah waited for the lift to take her back to her room.

★　★　★

Half an hour later there was a tap on her door.

'Hannah, you've missed all the drama!' Tess was breathless as she followed her inside.

'What's happened?'

'Nick and Claudia have just had a big row out on deck. Everyone was watching. She lashed out at him and he had to restrain her. It happened just now as I was coming up to see you.'

Hannah felt her hands go clammy and her heart began to thump.

'Evidently he went ashore without

telling her and she was furious.'

Tess stopped and gave her a concerned look. 'Hannah, are you all right?'

'Just tired. Think I'll have a lie down.'

'It's probably the heat. Look, I have to fly. I have clients waiting. What I came to ask you was if you fancy a drink in the Skylight Bar before dinner? About six? I should be finished by then.'

'Yes, that would be good. I'll see you there,' she said as she saw Tess out.

However, she didn't stay in her cabin and rest after Tess had left. She was far too wound up for that now, so she took the lift to the very top deck which was usually quiet at this time of day. She simply couldn't face the confines of her room with so much whirring round in her head.

Leaning on the smooth wooden rail looking out across the bay, the rhythm of the sea began to calm her. The air was warm with a slight breeze, the sky a clear crystal blue. Boats were moving around the harbour making ripples on the water that glinted brightly in the sunlight. Gradually the confusion in her head began to clear.

Gary had told her Nick had never settled down. It explained a lot. He'd have gone home after that cruise and had second thoughts about the commitment he'd made to her. He would have looked back on their three weeks together and seen it for what it was, just another flirtation with another woman on another ship. It must have happened all the time and she had been naïve to think their brief time together would have meant anything more to him. He'd obviously not given her a second thought. Now the same thing was happening again, this time with Claudia.

Hannah returned to her cabin, showered and dressed in a short cream dress. She took trouble with her hair and make-up, then made her way to the bar to meet Tess for that drink.

The Skylight bar was quiet with just a few people dotted around relaxing over their drinks and listening to a string quartet playing gentle music.

Hannah loved this room with its cream walls, soft lighting and floral arrangements in every corner.

There was no sign of Tess at the central bar. Then she spotted her sitting by one of the huge picture windows overlooking the bay. Tess smiled when she saw her and indicated the two large glasses of wine she had lined up on the low, round table. Hannah joined her and sank into one of the plush chairs opposite.

The evening was perfect, with the sun beginning to dip in a scarlet-streaked sky.

'So how was St Tropez?' Tess asked after elaborating on all the happenings of the afternoon.

'It was good. We took a boat trip round the bay, had a drink in a bar and mooched round the little narrow streets. Gary's so easy to be with. We really enjoyed ourselves.'

Hannah was determined to keep the conversation light and put the trauma of the day completely out of her mind.

Tess turned her head towards the bar. 'Look who's just come in — and she's heading our way.'

Hannah didn't need to look. The nice cosy chat she had been looking forward to wasn't going to happen now. Of all the people on board, Claudia was the last person she wanted to see!

Claudia cast a cool gaze over Hannah as she placed the large glass of wine she'd brought over on the table in front of them and then eased herself into the sofa beside Tess.

'Well, have you made up with you-know-who?' Tess asked her.

'He's just being difficult,' she told Tess, completely ignoring Hannah.

'Oh, how inconvenient,' Tess said sarcastically.

'I think he needs a break. He's so offhand with me at the moment. I don't seem to be able to get through to him.'

'Well, at least you know where he is. He can't get up to much trouble in the galley,' Tess said.

'He'd better not,' Claudia said with a

raised eyebrow. 'But that's the problem. He won't come out of it. Says he's busy. Then when he does get time off, what does he do? Goes waltzing off ashore without even telling me. I don't know what's got into him.'

'Maybe he's hiding from you,' Tess quipped.

Claudia didn't look pleased. 'Well, he can hide away all he likes. See if I care!'

The conversation continued with Claudia ignoring Hannah. Not that Hannah minded. She wouldn't have joined in the conversation even if Claudia had given her a chance.

'You'd better get rid of the fellow you were draped round last night in the Hub,' Tess joked.

Claudia gave a wry smile. 'Maybe.'

'Behave yourself. If lover-boy does decide to appear you could find yourself in a tricky situation.'

'I'll cope,' Claudia said taking a large slurp from her glass of wine.

'I don't know how you manage to get away with it,' Tess said.

'Treat 'em mean, keep 'em keen,' Claudia said with a wink. She stood and picked up her glass. 'Well, I'll take this back to my room and leave you two to your chat,' she said, giving Hannah a withering look.

'You've gone quiet,' Tess said once Claudia had gone. 'You don't like Claudia, do you?'

'Does it show?'

'Just a bit,' Tess laughed. 'She takes a bit of getting used to, I admit, but we all have to rub along on a ship, don't we?'

'Of course.' Hannah knew it was true. She had to pull herself together. Claudia had left them now. She and Tess were free to enjoy their drink and chat together. She took a deep breath, managed a smile and felt a lot calmer.

'Well, Calvi tomorrow,' Tess sighed. 'I love that place. I often thought I'd like to live there.'

'Yes, it's one of the places I really want to see. All the passengers were over the moon about it last time I was here but I couldn't get ashore. We were booked up all day for the gala dinner.'

'Tell me about it! I can't remember when I last went ashore. The joys of working on board.'

'You'll have to do what I've done and take a cruise yourself.'

'That's not a bad idea. Maybe I will one day.' She paused, then added, 'Are you going ashore with Gary again tomorrow?'

'I don't know, he didn't say anything about it.'

'I expect he'll want to go with his mum. She didn't go into St Tropez, did she? I saw her out on deck and she said she just wanted to relax and enjoy being on board.'

'I think she doesn't want Gary to feel he has to look after her all the time.'

'He's a great guy, so kind to everyone. He'd make someone a lovely husband.'

Hannah smiled and agreed.

They chatted on until Tess said she wanted to get her feet up. 'I'm going to grab a sandwich and have a lazy evening. I haven't sat down all day.'

Hannah was hungry and decided she would go into the main restaurant tonight and enjoy the luxury of being served a three-course dinner. It was a daunting prospect on her own but she was determined to be brave and face up to it.

4

The restaurant was brightly lit with tables set formally between huge mirrored columns. Almost every table was taken, with groups of people laughing and chatting as waiters took orders and served bottles of wine and plates of food. Hannah had never eaten in the restaurant when she'd worked on ships. The crew always ate in the staff dining room or the buffet bars.

She stood uncertainly viewing the room and was about to retreat when a waiter came up to her and asked if she wanted a table for one. He was looking to see where he could place her when Nick came striding up to him.

'I'll sort this one out,' he said. The waiter looked puzzled but nodded and walked back to the entrance where other diners were waiting to be seated.

Hannah felt self-conscious standing

there while Nick searched the room for a suitable table for her. Then Hannah spotted Nancy waving vigorously from the far end.

'I'll join Gary over there,' she told Nick and edged past him in order to walk over to where Gary and his mum were sitting.

'Oh, very well then,' he said, in an off-hand manner and was already striding away. His jaw had tensed and she knew he wasn't pleased but she wasn't going to let Nick decide how she spent her time on board or who she spent it with.

Gary stood up and pulled out a chair for her to sit. 'I came looking for you earlier to ask if you wanted to join us but you weren't in your cabin.'

'I went up to the Skylight Bar with Tess,' Hannah replied, putting all thoughts of Nick from her mind.

'Never mind, you're here now,' Nancy said, patting her hand. 'And I believe you've had a lovely day, the two of you.'

Hannah smiled.

'You should come with us next time.'

'Well, I will tomorrow. I want to see Calvi. I've heard what a lovely island Corsica is. And we've booked the coach to L'Île Rousse. Are you going on that outing?'

'No, I've only booked one. They're a bit expensive. I thought I'd just wander round Calvi.'

'I expect there's plenty to see in the town, dear. Sometimes we miss what's right in front of our noses by trying to do too much,' Nancy said.

Gary ordered more wine and recommended the pork, for which Hannah was grateful — she hated ploughing through huge menus.

When dinner was over Nancy said she would retire to her room. Gary pulled the chair out for Hannah to get up, then put a hand to her back as he guided her from the restaurant. Once out on deck Nancy said goodnight and left them together.

'What do you fancy doing now?' Gary asked.

'It's a beautiful evening. Why don't we sit out here on deck for a while? It seems a shame to go inside and miss the sunset.'

'You're such an old romantic!' Gary teased. She felt herself blush. 'But there's nothing wrong with that,' he was quick to reassure her.

The ship was gently gliding towards Corsica and as they watched, the sun set the sky ablaze over the still, dark water Hannah thought she had rarely seen anything so stunning.

Astern of them the lights of St Tropez reflected in the harbour and the honey-coloured buildings glowed warmly in the fading light.

Half an hour later Gary got up and said he'd go and check on his mum. Hannah smiled up at him, content to stay put and relax in the cool of the evening, alone with her thoughts as she watched the sun finally dip down below the horizon.

★ ★ ★

It was much later, as she turned to go back inside, that she saw Nick watching her from the far side of the deck, his face shadowy in the moonlight. He looked a little uncertain as he came towards where she was standing.

'I'm sorry about before in the restaurant.'

'It's OK. I just didn't want to eat alone.'

'I realised that, but I shouldn't have just left you standing there. I'm afraid I wasn't in the best of moods.' He gave a wry smile. 'I'm sure you've heard about it.'

'Tess said Claudia had been making trouble.'

'And I was the cause of it. Went ashore without telling her and she was furious with me.'

'And why did you do that?' Part of her didn't want this conversation yet she needed to know.

He shrugged. 'Just wanted to get away for a while, really.'

'Away from Claudia?'

77

He sighed deeply. 'Yes.'

'That's not a good sign when you're thinking of settling down together.'

He frowned. 'Where did you get that idea?'

'That's what she was telling Tess.'

'Well, she's got it wrong. I'm not thinking of settling down with Claudia or anyone else. I'll have to have words with her and put her straight.'

'Well, don't involve me.'

He shook his head. 'Claudia's behaviour isn't because of you. It's me. I'm not behaving the way she wants me to.'

'But you told me you weren't in a relationship.'

'We're not.' There was a shift in his expression as if he were considering what to say next. 'I've been trying to let her down gently but it's not working,' he said eventually.

'From what I've heard, Claudia usually gets what she wants.'

'Not from me,' he said in a determined voice.

They stood looking at each other

until it became uncomfortable.

'Did you enjoy St Tropez?' he said finally, to break the silence.

'Yes, I did. I was surprised to see you there,' she said, relieved the subject had been dropped.

'We do get *some* time off,' he smiled, back to his usual good humour.

'But you disappeared. Gary was hoping to have a chat with you.'

'It wasn't Gary I was hoping to spend time with,' he said, giving her a meaningful look.

She quickly turned away and they stood for some time looking out across the dark ocean, both lost for words.

Music began to drift up from a lower deck where a quartet of musicians had set up beside the floodlit pool. Deck lights illuminated a young woman in a long black dress who had positioned herself in front of the microphone. She began to sing a love song, one she and Nick had danced to on board that first ship.

They both turned to face each other at the same moment. Warm eyes met hers and for a moment the pain in her heart was quelled.

'Hannah, I'm sorry I couldn't go through with it. It was wrong of me to let it slide. I should have explained how I felt.'

'It's all in the past,' she said, trying to keep her voice steady.

'I wish it wasn't,' he said regretfully.

There were things she needed to tell him, things he ought to know, yet she couldn't find the words.

After several moments of silence he turned and walked away towards the far end of the deck where he paused and looked far out towards the horizon. Eventually he disappeared down onto a lower deck and she was left staring after him, her heart full of sadness.

The cool evening air soothed her as she wandered towards the stern of the ship and stood mesmerised by the white foam in the churning water as it glided slowly towards Corsica. Above, stars twinkled in the vast expanse of the universe.

Gently floating through her mind was

the memory the music had evoked. The joy of being in Nick's arms when it all began, the warmth and comfort his presence had given her, the words he had spoken, the expectations . . . that last evening that had held so much promise. The promise of love that was never to be fulfilled.

She had to phone Josie; talking to her sister would take her mind off these melancholy thoughts. Walking quickly back to her cabin she was already dialling the number.

'Hi, Hannah. How's the cruise? Is it living up to expectations?'

'It seemed strange at first but I'm getting used to being a passenger. It's nice to be waited on.'

'Well, that's what you went for.'

'How's Charlie?'

'Fine. He's been to a birthday party today, one of his nursery school friends. I stayed with him and it was bedlam! Twelve four-year-olds rampaging around the garden — and Charlie was the noisiest of them all.'

Hannah felt herself welling up.

'So, he's not missing me then?'

Josie chuckled. 'Not so you'd notice.'

'Well, give him a big kiss from his mum.'

Hannah told her about the ship and St Tropez. Josie filled her in on the latest in her divorce proceedings and how Charlie's antics were helping to make it all bearable.

Gradually Nick began to fade from her mind.

★   ★   ★

They sailed into Calvi early next morning while Hannah was breakfasting out on deck. A pink haze hovered above the water, making the sky and sea merge to a pale blue. As they passed the Citadel high on the promontory rock its cream stone walls began to glow in the morning light. Built as a fortification centuries ago, it now stood at the entrance to the harbour welcoming visitors to the port. All around them small boats tacked into the wind and larger vessels moved slowly towards their moorings.

As the Bel Rosa slid into the harbour and moored offshore, the town came into view with its cream-coloured buildings set against forest covered mountains. Hannah's pulse began racing at the thought of exploring this beautiful island.

While she was getting ready to go down to the gangway, there was a knock on her door.

Gary stood outside in the alleyway.

'Hannah, there's a spare place on the coach today. Mum was at the desk when Eleanor said Bryn wasn't feeling up to it and could she cancel his place. So Mum said you might like to take it.' He paused waiting for her answer. 'You remember Bryn. The old chap who was talking to my mum at the sailing party, and his quiet little wife, Eleanor.'

Hannah nodded. 'Yes, of course.'

His smile faded. 'Look, don't feel you have to, but you know what Mum's like. She's a bit of a busybody and she wouldn't let off until I said I'd come and ask you. Only, it leaves in an hour's time. So if you fancy joining us I'll let them know. It's all paid for so it wouldn't cost you anything.'

Hannah was wondering if she really should accept this offer and wishing she hadn't said anything about it being too expensive. Part of her was looking forward to a day on her own away from the ship, free to explore. Yet this tour round the island with a visit to the town of L'Île Rousse was one she had coveted but knew on her budget she wouldn't be able to afford.

As Gary gabbled on, he began to look more and more uncomfortable, almost apologetic for bothering her. She quickly pulled herself together.

'Gary, I'd love to come. Tell your mum thank you.'

He looked relieved. 'You want to . . . really?'

'I just said so,' she laughed.

As she gathered her things together in her room she smiled happily to herself at the prospect of a day with Nancy and Gary away from the ship. As it was to be a coach tour, there would be no risk of another difficult encounter with Nick.

When she arrived at the gangway Nancy was chatting with Eleanor among the others who were waiting on deck for the tender that would take them from their moorings to the quay. Gary was watching out for her and was soon at her side.

'Mum's taken Eleanor under her wing, as you can see,' Gary said with a smile.

'That's nice of her. Especially as she was stuck talking to her husband at the sailing party.'

'I think Mum feels sorry for Eleanor having to put up with Bryn.'

'If anyone can cheer her up, your mum will.'

'Mum's like that. She'll look after her all day.'

Eleanor looked about the same age as Nancy, a quiet, shy little woman with pretty blonde hair curling round her face.

'She always looks so nervous,' Gary said.

Hannah nodded in agreement. 'I have the feeling Eleanor would rather be any-where than here without her husband.'

'Anyway, let's go and join them, give Mum some moral support.'

'I'm sorry about your husband,' Hannah said to Eleanor.

Eleanor turned to her, a frown creasing her face. 'Yes, I wasn't sure whether I should come or not, but Bryn insisted, although I'd really rather have stayed on board with him.'

'Don't worry,' Nancy assured her. 'I'm sure Bryn will be fine. And you can spend the day with us. We'll look after you.'

Eleanor gave a nervous smile. It was difficult to know what she was thinking as she said little.

The tender arrived and soon had them speeding across the harbour towards the quay. Once ashore they strolled along the Quay Landry with its quaint stone houses, cafés, bars and shops, facing a beach of fine white sand and gently lapping water.

The coach was parked at the far end and Nancy took the seat beside Eleanor, leaving Gary free to sit with Hannah. It was a short drive to the little town of L'Île Rousse. The driver gave a running commentary but Hannah hardly listened as she stared out of the window at the scenery . . . plane trees with their elegant grey trunks and delicate green leaves wafting gently in the breeze, then olive groves set against pine-covered mountains tinged golden by the morning sunlight.

The coach parked just outside the town to allow them to walk along the beach. When they turned into its shady, narrow streets Gary strode ahead with Hannah but kept checking that Nancy and Eleanor were still following, waiting every now and then for them to catch up.

Hannah loved the slow pace of the island with cars moving round people and everything so laid back. It seemed like the sort of seaside place you saw in old photos, safe and peaceful.

Eventually Nancy insisted they stop at one of the pavement cafés in the square for coffee.

'You two carry on if you want to,' she told Gary. 'But I'm ready for a sit down.' She looked to Eleanor who nodded.

'I fancy a coffee too,' Hannah said, spotting a table under a shady awning. A waiter appeared almost immediately and Gary ordered the drinks.

'I hope Bryn will have recovered when you get back,' Nancy said.

'It depends whether he wins or not,' Eleanor mumbled, looking rather embarrassed. 'He hates losing, you see.'

'Losing what?'

'The bridge match.'

'But I thought you said he was ill.'

'Yes, that's what he told me to say.'

'So he's not ill, then?' Gary put in, surprised.

'Not really.' Eleanor was getting more flustered.

'I'm a pretty good hand at bridge

myself,' Gary said, trying to spare her any more embarrassment. 'Maybe he'll give me a game sometime.'

'Oh, no, he wouldn't do that,' Eleanor shot back. 'He's a grand master, you know.'

Gary looked taken aback, then shrugged and smiled pleasantly.

Nancy commented on the statue she could see from where they were sitting and Hannah got up to read the inscription. Then it was time to go back to the coach.

'That was a strange conversation,' Gary whispered to Hannah.

'There's definitely something wrong there. She seems almost afraid of him.'

They didn't pursue the conversation as Eleanor and Nancy were in the seats behind them.

On the way back the coach stopped in a lovely forested area with a short walk down to a pretty cove. Nancy and Eleanor went in search of an ice cream while Hannah and Gary padded across the soft sand and slipped their shoes off to paddle in the cool water.

'What a lovely island,' Gary said as they stood watching sunlight dance on the ripples.

'I'm rather glad Bryn didn't come. He would have spoiled the day.'

'But did you see how Eleanor began to shake when she spoke about him?' Gary said.

'Yes, I did. It made me feel uncomfortable.'

'She's so nervous and jumpy, and looks on the point of tears when she mentions him.'

'It's as if she wants to tell us something but doesn't know how.'

'But we can't just barge in and ask her, though, can we?'

'Maybe she'll open up to your mum. She's the sort of person I'd talk to if I had a problem.'

Gary gave her a questioning look.

'Do you have a problem?'

'No, not at all. I was just saying . . . '

Gary had obviously got wind of something. Maybe he and Nick had been talking. She couldn't ask him outright but it made her feel uncomfortable.

Again Gary gave her a searching look, then he smiled. 'Ah, well, at least it meant you could come instead.' He reached to take her hand as they padded along the sand. It seemed such a natural thing to do and settled the awkward moment between them. She trusted Gary, and whatever was going on behind the scenes she knew he would always act honourably.

She smiled up at him. 'Thanks, Gary. I've really enjoyed today. It was kind of you to ask me.'

Nancy and Eleanor were waiting for the tender to take them back to the ship. As there seemed no sign of it arriving, Gary wandered off to look at the boats.

'Shall we sit at that beach café and wait for it?' Nancy suggested.

'I wouldn't mind a cup of tea,' Eleanor murmured and Hannah readily agreed.

Sipping her tea, Nancy sighed.

'It's been a lovely day.'

She glanced at Eleanor who was again looking strained, her face creased with anxiety. Nancy reached across and took her hand.

'I hope Bryn's in a better mood when you get back,' she said, and Hannah wondered if she had divulged anything of the problem to Nancy.

Eleanor forced a smile as she looked up at Nancy then her bottom lip began to quiver. She took a deep breath and said, 'I doubt it. I don't know why he puts up with me. I'm not much company, am I?' Eleanor shook her head. 'He's a good man, really, and he looks after me, but . . .'

'But what?' Nancy prompted gently.

'Well, it's just his manner. It's his army training, you know. He likes things done his way or he gets cross. It's easier just to go along with it, but sometimes I can't get it right, and then . . .'

There was a stunned silence while Nancy and Hannah glanced at each other, not knowing what to say. Eleanor fidgeted with a tissue she'd just dabbed her eyes with. There seemed nothing they could do that would make it any better so Nancy just held her hand until her tears had dried then uttered words of comfort until she managed to bring a smile to her face.

* * *

Hannah couldn't help worrying about Eleanor as she climbed the gangway back into the ship. There was definitely something wrong. It played on her mind as she tidied her cabin and prepared to have a shower. Maybe they'd had a falling out. Most couples did from time to time. As she stood under the warm refreshing water she decided there was nothing she could do about it so it wasn't worth worrying.

She was tired after the day out, but she was hungry. The Poolside Grill would be her best bet. She wouldn't need to dress up and could grab a pizza and some salad and eat it at one of the deck tables in front of the bar. She pulled on a pair of cotton trousers and a fresh top, bundled her hair into a ponytail and slipped her feet into some comfy sandals. It would do for tonight. She had no intention of socialising.

5

The poolside grill was quiet but for one couple sharing a bottle of wine and a salad. Hannah looked over the deck just in case Nick was around, then ordered her pizza. Sitting on a raffia chair at one of the shiny steel tables she watched as the chef beneath his striped canopy bounced dough from hand to hand as if performing on stage.

When she saw Tess coming down the steps beside the bar, she felt herself relax. She wouldn't have to eat a lonely dinner after all. Tess waved to Hannah and ordered a pizza for herself, then joined her at the table.

'So how was Calvi?' Tess asked as she put her glass of wine on the table and pulled out a seat opposite to Hannah.

'It was a strange afternoon.' She told Tess about Eleanor and how worried they had all been.

'Poor woman,' Tess said. 'I don't think I've come across her. Tell her to come and have a nice relaxing massage. That'll make her feel better.'

'What, and let Claudia loose on her?' Hannah said jokingly.

Tess sighed. 'Don't speak to me about that one. She's been a pain all day. We can't shut her up about her wonder boyfriend, Nick.'

Hannah immediately regretted introducing Claudia into the conversation.

'I thought they were fighting yesterday,'

'Oh, they're like that all the time. He does something that displeases her, she rants and raves at him, he shrugs it off, then when she's calmed down she's nice to him again. Poor old Nick has a dog's life with her.'

'She had her arms draped round another man in the nightclub,' Hannah said. Then she wondered why she'd said something so bitchy and kept the conversation about Claudia going.

'That doesn't surprise me. She

always has a man in tow. But evidently Nick's the man of the moment again.'

'So why does he put up with it?' Hannah could feel pain cutting through her yet she couldn't stop herself from finding out more.

Tess shrugged. 'She's the type men like — slim, blonde, attractive — she's got it all.'

Hannah stared down at the pizza the chef had placed in front of her. Tess was right. With his looks and personality Nick could have his pick of women. So why would he ever have bothered with someone like her? How could she have been so naïve as to believe his words of love?

'I'm going to finish this, then have a quiet read in my cabin,' she said, hoping her voice did not betray her emotions.

'It's Sète tomorrow,' Tess sighed. 'Another place I'd like to see. It's supposed to be like Venice, criss-crossed with canals.'

'I've booked a coach trip out to the

Chateau,' Hannah said, feeling a slight uplifting of her spirits at the thought of the day ahead.

'Lucky you! Everyone I've spoken to has said how good that one is.'

Tess finished her pizza and got up. 'Ah, well, at least I'm finished for today so it's a hot shower and an early night for me.'

★   ★   ★

Once inside her cabin Hannah felt restless. She couldn't sit all evening moping, knowing everyone else was out there enjoying themselves. Yet she couldn't face wandering round the ship looking for something to do. Sitting on the bed staring at the wall, she wished she was safe at home, with Josie in the flat below, always ready to lend a sympathetic ear.

Searching frantically in her bag, she pulled out her phone with shaking hands while silently praying that Josie would answer.

'Nick's on the ship,' she blurted out

as soon as she heard her sister's voice.

There was silence for a moment then Josie's voice came through calm and comforting.

'Hannah, you sound upset. What's happened?'

'Nothing, but I was hoping we wouldn't come in contact but he seems to be following me round.'

'Have you spoken?'

'Briefly.' There was a tremble in her voice.

'Did he explain why he didn't keep in touch?'

'He said he couldn't go through with it.'

'And he didn't have the guts to tell you? Did you tell him about Charlie?'

'No.'

'Are you going to?'

'No, I don't want him to know.'

'Very wise. He doesn't deserve to know. And it might cause complications.'

Hannah was fighting with her emotions.

'You're right, of course, it's just that I

feel awkward seeing him after what happened.'

'Do you still have feelings for him?' Josie ventured.

'I suppose so . . . I don't know how I feel.'

'What about him?'

'He's got a girlfriend on board.'

'In that case, leave well alone. Avoid them. It shouldn't be impossible on a ship that size,' Josie said firmly. 'You know how he upset you last time. You don't want all that again.'

'I know.'

'Good, now let's forget about Nick and tell me about the cruise. Are you having a good time?'

'Yes, Gary's here. I sailed with him a couple of times before. And so is Tess. Remember I told you about her?'

'Sounds like it's a reunion! Now you forget about Nick and concentrate on enjoying yourself. He's not worth spoiling your holiday for.'

Hannah put the phone back in her bag determined to do exactly what Josie said. On a ship this size it should be possible to avoid Nick.

Forgetting about him was harder, but she had to try.

It was still early, and there was a music and dance show on in the theatre and the group playing in the Hub later tonight was one she liked. If she kept her mind occupied it should help.

She changed into loose trousers and a pretty top, brushed her tangled hair into submission and put on a touch of make-up. Strolling down the alleyway towards the lifts she felt confident she could do this.

The theatre was all smooth shapes in cream and gold, with gentle concealed lighting and tiers of deep blue seating in a semicircle in front of a stage draped in heavy gold curtains. It was packed when Hannah got there but she managed to find a seat beside an elderly couple who gave her a friendly smile and made her feel welcome.

Gentle music came through loud-speakers to create an atmosphere of expectation as Hannah settled into the plush velvet seat and breathed a sigh of contentment. At least once the show started, she could relax into the darkness.

An explosion of music announced the show was to begin. As the curtains parted a troupe of dancers came onto the stage. The whole show was a spectacle of light and colour as one scene followed another, each more spectacular than the previous one. Hannah was transported into other worlds as the music washed over her and the rhythm of the dances had her feet tapping.

Finally the curtain came down on a stage bathed in glorious golden light as the audience erupted into applause.

When she came out dusk, was settling over the ship but the air was still balmy. The Hub wouldn't have got into full swing yet so she decided to go out on deck for a while and enjoy the night air. Bow waves lapped the sides of the ship as it made steady progress to the port of Sète. Moonlight danced on the ripples, making them sparkle and a peace settle over her.

She and Nick had strolled out on deck on a night like this and he had taken her in his arms and held her close. It all seemed so long ago . . .

Music reached her ears as she approached the Hub. Pausing at the entrance, she viewed the group on stage and decided she would enjoy listening to them. The bar at the far end was lit with Tiffany lamps giving a warm glow. If she could find a seat and order a drink it should be possible to sit quietly without feeling conspicuously alone.

Unfortunately there were no seats left and the bar was crowded. Then one of the gentlemen offered a stool, which she accepted gratefully. It was tucked away at the end of the bar with a view of the musicians and the dance floor but where she felt comfortably unobserved. Settling onto its smooth leather top, she ordered a glass of wine from the barman.

Dance music resonated round the

room and her feet began to twitch. A few couples were moving slowly on the floor in front of the group. Her thoughts turned to the times she had danced with Nick and the joy she'd felt. It was about the only time they had been able to get together, once the salon had closed and the galley was quiet.

'I thought I might find you in here. It's your sort of music.'

His voice brought her out of her reverie and she turned from staring down at her drink to find Nick standing beside her.

'I was just having a nightcap before bed,' she said, trying to keep her tone light. She knew this wasn't going to be as easy as Josie had predicted.

Nick ordered a beer from the barman and chatted with him briefly, then turned to Hannah.

'We spent many a happy hour dancing the night away, didn't we?'

'Yes, we did.'

'I often think about the time we were together.'

Hannah wanted to ask him why he hadn't done something about it instead of just thinking, but the words wouldn't come. The gentle music, the softly glowing lamps, the whole atmosphere was so romantic she couldn't bear to spoil it. She turned away from him and picked up her glass of wine.

Strains of *Our Love Is Here To Stay* came through the microphone in pure, clear tones and brought a lump to Hannah's throat. They had listened to it on the last night they had been together. He had murmured in her ear that the words belonged to them. He had promised their love would last, and she had believed him.

When his hand reached out to take hers, all sensible thought deserted her and she slid off the bar stool to take it. Nick had clearly stated that he and Claudia were not in a relationship and she wanted to believe him. Nick guided her through the throng of people onto the small dance floor and they filtered in among the other couples. He took her in his arms and began to move slowly beneath a glitter ball of rotating light as the singer softly crooned on. It was as if the years had fallen away and she was where she belonged.

'I'm going to have to leave you for a moment,' Nick said suddenly, and abruptly disentangled himself from her. She stood in a daze as he walked away. Then she saw Claudia. The woman was looking up at him angrily. They spoke briefly then left together.

Hannah stood mortified, unable to believe what had happened! It seemed like a bad dream. After several minutes, she managed to get back to the bar, slithered onto the bar stool and ordered a large glass of wine. Tears sprang to her eyes and she brushed them away. How could he have done that to her?

Later she made it up to her cabin as guilt and anguish began to consume her. She could hardly believe she had allowed it to happen.

Dejectedly she prepared for bed and, after much heart-searching, fell into a fitful sleep, desperately wishing the whole thing had been a bad dream.

★ ★ ★

The coach was parked on the quay early next morning. Hannah settled in a window seat trying to empty her mind of last night's events.

When Linda came striding along the aisle, Hannah lifted her bag to make room for her, glad of any distraction that would take her mind off the nightmare she was still living through.

'You don't mind, do you?' Linda said. 'I don't want to be stuck with some man, and there are several singles on this coach.'

'Any man in particular?' Hannah said, forcing cheerfulness into her voice.

'They're all the same. Bore the life out of you. Always on about sport and trying to impress you.' She turned to Hannah. 'You won't do that, will you?'

Hannah felt the weight in her chest lighten in Linda's company. 'I haven't the least interest in sport,' she reassured her.

'I'm into chess. Do you call that sport? Not keen on running about or getting wet.'

The mention of chess made Hannah think of Eleanor. 'Have you played on board at all?' Hannah ventured.

Linda shook her head. 'Not had time. I can do that at home. I want to make the best of all the things we can see on the cruise.' She raised an eyebrow. 'What makes you ask? It sounds like a loaded question.'

'You're very observant. And yes, it is.' Hannah told Linda about Eleanor.

Linda tutted. 'Beats me how any woman can take that sort of treatment. I'd be off like a shot!'

'Maybe we're reading too much into it, but she seems so nervous and on edge all the time. Every time Bryn is mentioned she gets flustered and weepy. There must be something to make her like that.'

'I shouldn't worry about it. There's

nothing you can do. She has to sort it herself.'

Hannah nodded. 'You're right. Oh, look, we're here! There's the chateau in front of us.'

Once off the coach they trundled up the steps of the chateau where the Count welcomed them. He seemed a jovial sort and after a short introduction in one of the stately rooms, he had them climbing the grand staircase with its many oil paintings and into bedrooms complete with tapestry wall hangings and four-poster beds.

Next they were taken on a guided tour of the grounds. Linda was keen to keep at the front so she didn't miss any of commentary while Hannah was happy trailing near the back of the group absorbing the beauty of her surroundings as they strolled through olive groves and vineyards, admiring the French-style gardens and the terraced flower beds.

The tour of the chateau ended in a lovely bamboo grove where seats had been laid out for a session of wine tasting. The Count explained the characteristics of each wine the estate produced while his young sons handed round small glasses for them to sample.

On leaving the chateau, the coach took them to Montpellier where they had a couple of hours to look round, then back to Sète by way of the lovely lagoons and canals that characterised the area.

Back in the harbour, Linda suggested they have a look round the town and Hannah agreed.

'Do you live on your own?' Linda asked, as they settled in one of the cafés by the harbour.

'Yes, I do. I gather you're on your own, too.'

'Absolutely. Wouldn't have it any other way.'

'Never been tempted?' Hannah ventured.

'Never. My parents argued all the time. It was enough to put anyone off. I vowed that I would never get into that situation. How about you?'

'I've had a few relationships but none that worked out,' Hannah replied.

'Would you have liked them to?' Linda pushed.

'Well, there was one . . . '

Linda gave her a searching look then shook her head. 'You've had a close escape, then. Men are simply not worth the trouble. Better on your own.'

Hannah nodded but gave no answer.

★   ★   ★

Bryn and Eleanor were out on deck watching the tender draw close to the ship. On her way up to her room, Hannah bumped into them.

'Why don't you join me for a drink before dinner?' Hannah directed the question to Eleanor. She didn't know why she had suggested such a thing, as she was sure Bryn wouldn't like it, but felt she needed the distraction.

Eleanor gave her a doubtful look and turned to Bryn. He seemed in good spirits and agreed.

She watched them disappear into the accommodation and then wondered what to do next. Food was uppermost in her mind as she hadn't eaten since breakfast; there hadn't been time with all the sight-seeing. If she went straight up to the Windsor Room she should just be in time for a proper afternoon tea.

Back in her room, she pulled a brush through her hair and slipped into a fresh shirt, slung her bag over her shoulder and trotted along to the lift. She'd shower and dress for the evening later.

It was with some apprehension she approached the Windsor Room, knowing it would be quite formal and a little intimidating. Nervously viewing the scene from the entrance, she saw people seated at small round tables. Silver teapots glistened among the fine china, all laid out on crisp white linen. It looked welcoming and friendly. Her doubts dispelled, she walked confidently in.

A smiling waiter escorted her to a window seat with two comfy chairs and a wonderful view of the harbour. Almost instantly another waiter came with a tray of tea, followed by another bearing dainty sandwiches. Feeling hungry, she knew she could do justice to anything on offer!

A wonderful feeling of calm came over her as she gazed through the window at the still blue water and relaxed into a welcome cup of tea. The pianist was playing well-known melodies and the passengers were chatting.

The waiter returned as soon as she had emptied her plate and asked if she would like cake. Glancing round the room while she waited for it to arrive, she saw Nick. Standing there in his uniform, tall and straight with his smooth tanned skin, fair hair and pale blue eyes, he looked incredibly handsome and despite her best intentions her heart began beating a little faster.

He was absorbed in conversation with one of the waiters just inside the doorway. As if on cue he looked round the room and their eyes met.

It seemed a lifetime before he turned again to the waiter and resumed their conversation. Hannah shrank into her chair and tried to concentrate on the view from the window. After what had happened in the Hub, she did not want a confrontation with him in such a public place.

The cakes arrived but remained untouched on her plate. She'd hardly been aware of it being placed there. Eventually she picked up the knife and cut a scone. It was warm and fresh and crumbly. She dug into the pot of jam and spread it on one of the halves and then placed a blob of cream on top . . . and then stared at it.

Still Nick talked on. She tried to take a bite of the scone. The next time she glanced in his direction he was walking over towards her. He didn't take his eyes off her as he pulled the chair opposite and sat facing her. He cleared his throat and ran a hand over his hair.

'Hannah.'

She sat looking at him, waiting.

'Last night — ' He stopped.

'Last night we danced together,' she finished.

'I think it was more than that,' he said.

Her heart was beating so fast she was sure he could hear it. He smiled awkwardly and she noticed his hands were shaking. There was a long pause during which time his eyes never left her.

'It was a mistake,' she said flatly.

'Why do you say that?'

'I'm surprised you have the nerve to ask.'

'Because I went off with Claudia,' he said.

She remained tight-lipped and silent as he seemed to be gathering courage to continue.

'I was going to come back and explain but then I got called away. One of the chefs had burned his hand and I had to see to it.'

'You don't have to explain.'

'Yes, I do. The way I left you. was unforgivable.'

'It was.'

His brow creased. 'I'm truly sorry.' He paused again and let out a long breath. 'She'd seen us together and she'd had too much to drink. I had to get her out before she could cause trouble.'

'Nick, I don't want excuses. Just keep away from me and sort it out with Claudia.'

'I'm trying to. There really is nothing between me and Claudia if that's what's worrying you.'

'Nothing is worrying me, except you following me round. I don't want to get involved.'

'You're not involved. The problem lies with Claudia and unfortunately I'm the one she's taking it out on.'

The waiter Nick had been talking to came over and took his attention away. After a brief conversation Nick turned to Hannah, a look of despair on his face.

'There's an emergency in the galley.' He got up then hesitated. 'Hannah, please believe me . . . '

As she watched him stride back to the entrance her mind was in turmoil. She wanted to believe what he was telling her but a little voice inside her was telling her she should not trust him.

6

Back in her cabin Hannah showered and dressed, all the time pondering what Nick had said. She supposed it was possible he had been avoiding trouble when he'd ushered Claudia out of the bar. She knew how volatile Claudia could be. But she couldn't understand why Nick felt so responsible for her bad behaviour when he kept stressing that there was nothing between them.

Finally she managed to put it all out of her mind and, forcing a spring into her step, went to meet Bryn and Eleanor in the bar.

They were already there, Eleanor in a blue silk two-piece, Bryn looking smart in a nicely cut suit.

'What would you like to drink?' he asked in a hearty voice. 'How about a gin and tonic? I'm afraid we're not into these fancy cocktails. If you have a drink, let it be a proper one, is what I say.'

Hannah happily went along with it as it was a drink she liked but Eleanor looked up at him with a pleading smile. 'I'd quite like to try a cocktail. They look rather nice . . . '

'No, dear, you don't know what they put in them. Better stick to what you know.'

Bryn ordered three gin and tonics and told the ladies to find a table near one of the large windows. The waiter brought the drinks over on a tray and Bryn followed.

'I hear you both had a good day ashore yesterday,' he said, lowering himself heavily into one of the plush chairs.

'Yes' Hannah said. 'How did the chess go?'

Bryn gave Eleanor a stern look. 'Now what have you been telling them?'

'I told them at reception you were ill and that was why you had to cancel,' Eleanor said, her chin beginning to tremble.

'Bit of a tummy upset,' he said to Hannah.

'It's what you told me to say,' Eleanor persisted meekly.

Bryn gave her a stern look. Eleanor opened her mouth, thought better of it and fell silent, sipping her drink and not looking at either of them.

'We all overindulge on holiday,' Hannah said, attempting to lighten the mood. 'I shan't be able to get into my clothes by the end of the week.'

'Hmm, yes,' Bryn grunted.

Hannah felt uncomfortable, fearing they were about to have a row. The atmosphere became charged as they sat in silence. To Hannah's relief Bryn quickly regained his composure and began to tell her about other cruises they'd been on. It seemed they were pretty comfortably off and holidayed regularly. But it was obvious Bryn made all the decisions.

'So what have you planned for tomorrow?' Hannah asked Eleanor.

'We're staying on board tomorrow. There's a big match on,' Bryn answered for her.

'Looks like you'll have to go on your

own,' Hannah said, forcing a smile.

'Oh, no, I couldn't do that,' Eleanor said. 'Bryn wouldn't like it.'

'I let you go yesterday, didn't I?' he said in an aggrieved voice.

She gave him an almost defiant look. 'That was only because you wanted me out of the way.'

'It was because I wanted a bit of peace.'

Eleanor turned to Hannah. 'I would have liked to have gone today but Bryn wasn't keen.'

'Can't see why you'd want to. We come on cruises, my dear, to enjoy the ship, not to go wandering round a crumbling old chateau.'

'The chateau wasn't crumbling,' Hannah corrected him.

'I like looking at old buildings . . . ' Eleanor said, her voice trailing away.

'Well, we are not going ashore in Marseille tomorrow, that's for certain. I'm not getting involved with football hooligans.'

'It's only a televised match,' Hannah

said, his autocratic attitude beginning to annoy her.

'Maybe, but I'm not chancing it.' His tone made it clear that the conversation had ended. Eleanor pursed her lips and said no more.

Hannah was wondering how she could escape this awkward situation when Tess came rushing into the bar.

'Hannah, I've been looking for you all day! Some of us are going ashore for the evening. It's to an abbey for a meal and it's the most amazing place. You'd love it. We've got a minibus laid on and there's one place left. Do you fancy coming?'

Hannah's heart leapt for joy. It was just what she needed — a night out with her friend, away from the ship. Away from Nick. After a quick calculation she decided she could afford it as she'd spent little since joining the ship. And it definitely sounded worth splashing out on.

'I'd love to,' she said with enthusiasm.

'Great. Have to rush now. Got to change. See you by the gangway at seven.'

She watched Tess rush off and made her excuses for leaving Bryn and Eleanor.

'Sounds like you'll have a lovely evening,' Eleanor said somewhat enviously.

'Heard about that place,' Bryn muttered. 'Noisy and crowded. Not our sort of thing, dear.'

'No, I suppose it's more for the young ones.'

Hannah left them to go back to her cabin as it had already turned six and she wanted to make sure she looked her best for this night out.

★　★　★

An hour later she went down to the gangway to join the others. She hadn't had a chance to ask Tess what the dress code was but guessed it might be smart, so had put on her close-fitting black dress and high-heals. She breathed a sigh of relief when she saw the others were dressed up too.

Then she noticed Nick standing beside Claudia. She wore a low-cut dress and was flirting with him outrageously, although Nick seemed oblivious to her advances. It hadn't occurred to Hannah that they would be part of the group. Obviously they'd sorted out their differences. Hannah felt an overwhelming urge to run away, yet knew she couldn't. She just had to stick it out.

Tess was chatting with Gary. She hadn't expected him to be there either. There were several other couples she didn't know. At least she had two friends to keep her company, so she just had to try to ignore Nick and Claudia.

Tess came over to her and Gary followed.

'You look gorgeous,' he said.

A strange feeling of betrayal began to creep over her. Why hadn't Tess said anything about Gary going? And why hadn't Gary come for her as he had done on previous occasions?

'Wish my hair was as easy as yours,' Tess moaned. 'I spend hours trying to get it into a style and all you have to do is scrunch your curls on top of your head and it looks fabulous.'

Hannah forced a smile.

'Your hair always looks good, Tess.'

The compliments boosted Hannah's confidence but she couldn't shake off a feeling of disquiet at Tess and Gary appearing to be together. The whole atmosphere was wrong and she wished she hadn't come now.

'Hey, Nick, how did you get the night off? I thought they couldn't do without you,' one of the others shouted to him.

'Everything's going like clockwork in the galley. Ned's running the show just fine.'

Hannah watched in a daze as the scene unfolded around her. Then Nick turned and his eyes were searching hers. At that moment something passed between them, something that couldn't be denied. She turned away quickly, hoping the others hadn't noticed.

★   ★   ★

When they got on the minibus Gary insisted Hannah sit with Tess. They chatted all the way and Hannah began to relax.

Entering the abbey was like walking into another world. Minstrels in costume serenaded them with a variety of medieval musical instruments as they passed under an archway into a courtyard. Glasses of champagne and canapés were handed round as they stood in the shadow of the ancient abbey and listened to the music beneath the deepening blue of a twilight sky.

There was quite a walk to reach the dining area along arched cloisters where concealed lighting sent shadows over the ancient stone walls. Hannah had never been in such a magical place and gasped with pleasure at a tiny courtyard viewed through one of the arches where blue light illuminated a bubbling fountain at its centre.

The dining room was huge, its lofty arched roof illuminated with beams of brilliant blue light. An elaborate buffet stood at its centre, surrounded by long tables. Once seated, a waiter brought wine and invited them to help themselves to the elaborate display of food on offer.

It was a lively gathering, the huge lofty room filled with groups of people at all the long tables laughing and talking loudly. Hannah tried hard not to look at Nick, but because he was sitting with Claudia a little further down the table on the opposite side, it was difficult not to glance his way. He was in conversation with the person the other side of him most of the time and then would sit and stare at his food. Claudia kept trying to attract his attention but the only time Nick spoke to her was when she tugged at his arm and fluttered her eyelashes.

Throughout the meal two guitarists

in medieval costume circulated and serenaded each table in turn. As they approached their table Hannah averted her eyes, not wanting to be singled out. But the musicians came straight to her and stood beside her making her the focus of attention. Her cheeks were burning as they continued to strum gently on their guitars. Everyone's eyes were on her and she wished the floor would open up and swallow her. It seemed to go on interminably and she knew she wouldn't be able to stop the tears overflowing for much longer. It would be more than she could bear to create a scene in this packed room. Thankfully she managed to hold on just long enough before the musicians moved on to the next table. Then she didn't know where to look or what to say, so stared at her plate and pushed the food around on it.

When eventually she glanced up, Nick was looking straight at her, an unspoken dialogue passing between them that had all her senses responding. A ghost of a smile crossed his lips and then he was walking round the table toward her. Hannah hardly knew where to look. Her hands were clammy and the blood had drained from her face. Claudia was watching as Nick paused to say something to Gary as he passed him. Gary glanced in her direction. Tess gave her a worried look. Nick was almost with her now and Claudia was watching them closely.

Hannah knew there was going to be trouble yet felt helpless to avoid it. Nick must be mad to create such a scene in a place like this. All she could do was look mutely down at her plate, aware that everyone on the table was watching.

There was a spare chair at the end of the table next to her and Nick pulled it out and sat. Without a word he reached across the table and gently touched her fingers. She gave a silent gasp and quickly pulled away yet in that instant his touch had resonated through her whole body and set every nerve tingling.

'I think Claudia wants you back in

your place,' she said in an unsteady voice.

Hannah was aware of Claudia moving round the table towards them on unsteady legs and with a look of simmering hostility. A shiver of fear ran through her as she forced herself to watch the woman's progress. Time stood still. Hannah couldn't move, couldn't force herself to turn and look but sat quite still in her seat waiting.

'What are you doing over here?' Hannah heard her snap at Nick.

It all seemed surreal, as if it were taking place in slow motion and had nothing to do with her. Hannah felt an icy fear creep through her. Then she felt a sharp tap on the shoulder that brought her up rigid.

'What was that for?' Hannah's voice rose sharply as she got to her feet, a sudden rage forcing out her fear.

Claudia gave her a withering look. 'I saw how you looked at him,' she snarled. 'And I'd like to know just what's going on here.'

Hannah stepped back from the verbal assault and Nick grabbed Claudia's arm to guide her away. 'Come on, you've had too much to drink,' he said sternly.

Claudia gave a snort of derision and shrugged him off but was in no way equal to his strength and finally succumbed and let him lead her back to her place.

Hannah was left in a daze, hardly aware of what was going on around her. The huge choir that had taken to the stage were giving forth a rousing chorus amid much applause as blue strobe lighting lit the stage and illuminated the lofty arches of the roof. There was an encore, a quiet romantic ballad that instantly calmed the diners. Then the choir left the stage to thunderous applause and people began to move away from their tables. Gary shrugged into his jacket and helped Tess into hers. Hannah followed the others out into the cloisters.

Nick appeared beside her. 'I'm sorry for what happened. It was stupid of me, I know. I just needed to let you know how I felt. Claudia had no business acting the way she did. I didn't ask her to come with me. I didn't want her sitting by me. I don't even like her.'

Hannah continued walking, knowing she could not trust her voice to stay steady. 'Well, I wish you'd sort it out with her and leave me out of it,' she managed in a shaky voice.

Gary and Tess appeared and walked each side of her to where the minibus would pick them up to take them back to the ship. They chatted to each other beside her as they waited for the minibus to come.

Nick and Claudia were standing apart in silence and the others were huddled together. Everyone was tired and just wanted to get back on board. Hannah stood alone and was grateful for the darkness as she struggled to make sense of what had happened.

Back in the bus, Tess sat beside her but conversation was strained. Tess commented on Claudia's behaviour but Hannah couldn't respond. Eventually they fell silent. She was aware that everyone had witnessed Claudia's outburst and would know it had something to do with her and Nick. Well, she was beyond caring and just wanted her cabin and her bed. When the tender finally drew up alongside the ship, there were friendly farewells as they all trudged up the gangway and went their separate ways.

After an hour of trying to sleep Hannah gave up, pulled on some clothes and went out onto the deck. The ship was sailing now, leaving the twinkling lights of the port behind. In the distance a small boat bobbed on the choppy dark water. The night air was cool and she pulled her cardigan closer. The episode in the abbey had thoroughly shaken her. And there was something else disturbing her. Tess had been friendly, Gary had acted the perfect gentleman as usual and looked after both the girls. But she had sensed there was something developing between him and Tess. It shouldn't matter, but somehow it did.

After pacing the deck for some time turning everything over and over in her mind, she leaned on the rail at the side of the ship and watched the inky dark water of the harbour shimmering with reflections. The rhythm of the sea was calming as they sailed out into open waters. A shiver made her realise she was getting chilled, so she ambled back to her room. Once warm in her bed, tiredness enfolded her and finally she drifted into an uneasy sleep.

* * *

Next morning Hannah went for her usual buffet breakfast at the Terrace where she could sit out on deck and enjoy the early morning freshness before the heat of the day took over. It was a lovely bright morning. The sea was crystal clear, reflecting the deep blue of the sky.

Linda disturbed her solitude, pulling out a chair and plonking herself opposite. At first Hannah was reluctant but Linda was good company and she hadn't witnessed what had happened last night. Some banter might take her mind off it.

'Marseille, second largest city in France, oldest inhabited city in the Mediterranean, fourth largest port in Europe. Bouillabaisse is their speciality — fish stew to you and me. Must sample some,' Linda rattled off.

Hannah raised her eyebrows. 'Wow, somebody's been studying the guide book!'

Linda sat straight backed, guide book in hand. 'One hundred and sixty steps lead up to the ancient fortress which is the highest point in the city and on which stands the Basilica of Notre Dame. The old port is a favourite with tourists. There are museums and high-end shopping malls. Do you need more?'

'Phew, no thanks! Don't fancy all those steps.'

'Shall we stick with the shopping malls?' Linda said in a deadpan voice.

Hannah laughed. 'I might venture up

to the Basilica. I could do with some exercise after all this food.'

Linda shrugged. 'You're probably right. Waste of time shopping when there's so much to see. Think I'll go for a museum.'

As they sat over their coffee there was a stir among other diners. Some had got up and were moving towards the side of the ship. Linda jumped up then beckoned to Hannah.

'The pilot boat's coming alongside.'

Hannah joined her to peer down at the water just in time to see the pilot leap from the small moving boat onto the side of the ship. She held her breath as he scrambled up the vertical ladder and then disappeared inside the ship.

'Wow, he must be fit!' Hannah said.

They sat back at the table to finish their breakfast and the conversation turned again to Eleanor and Bryn.

'I met them in the bar for a drink last night and he seemed very domineering,' Hannah said. 'Whenever Eleanor speaks he shoots her down in flames. She seems frightened of him.'

'I wouldn't let any man rule me like that.'

'She should stand up to him,' Hannah agreed. 'But I suppose there's nothing we can do.'

'I'd have given him a piece of my mind.'

Hannah had no doubt that she would have done and was glad the situation had not arisen.

'Best leave them to it,' she said, getting up and preparing to leave.

7

As soon as the ship berthed in Marseille harbour Hannah headed for the gangway, anxious to see as much as she could of this ancient city. Nancy was in the lift and she was alone. Hannah asked where Gary was.

'Oh, he's still in bed. I knocked for him before I came down and got only a grunt as he peered out of the door. I think he had a late night.'

'Yes, we were late getting back to the ship.'

'Did you have a lovely time? It sounded like such a wonderful place.'

'You should have come with us,' Hannah said, trying not to get into any talk about what went on. She wasn't sure what Gary would have told her.

'Oh, I'm too old for that sort of thing. I'm going to bed when you youngsters are just going out.'

The lift stopped and they got out.

'Gary did come and tell me he was back on board. He knows I worry. But then he said he was going with Tess down to the Hub. These youngsters. Never know when to stop.'

So Gary and Tess *were* getting close. She should be pleased for them, but instead she felt somehow abandoned.

'Are you going ashore?' she asked Nancy, trying not to dwell on it.

'Yes, dear, I shall go and have a look round, but I won't stray far in case I get lost. Gary said he wouldn't bother with this port.'

'We could go together,' Hannah offered. If she had Nancy for company she wouldn't have time to think about Gary and Tess.

'Oh, I don't want to slow you down. I expect there are lots of things you want to see and I'm not as quick as I used to be.'

'We can go at your pace, no problem,' Hannah reassured her.

'Well, that's very kind of you, dear. I

would enjoy your company, and you can always sit me down with a cup of tea while you go off exploring.'

Hannah smiled and shook her head. 'It will probably be me that succumbs first. You could run circles round me.'

'Go on!' Nancy chuckled but she looked pleased that she was to spend the day with Hannah — and Hannah was glad of the company; she didn't want to spend the day alone.

It proved to be a lovely day. Nancy was game for anything. They walked to the Cathedral which was near to where the ship was berthed and then along the quay where the cruise ships were moored. It was a steep climb through many side streets to get to the Old Port and Nancy struggled with all the steps, but continued on bravely. The atmosphere there was lively with tourists milling along the quay.

They sat at one of the pavement cafés with views over the fishing harbour so Nancy could get her breath back, then browsed the gift shops.

Hannah wanted to see the Basilica but Nancy opted for a cup of tea while Hannah tackled all the steps. She was breathless by the time she reached the top but it was worth it for the view.

Back in the town they looked for a restaurant for lunch. 'We have to try the bouillabaisse,' Hannah said.

'Whatever's that?' Nancy asked in alarm.

'Fish stew. It's a speciality here. You'll love it.'

'Well, I like fish,' Nancy said, gamely. 'When in Rome and all that.'

Having found a pavement café that wasn't too busy, they ordered their food then sat quietly watching the scene about them while they waited for it to arrive.

'It's a pity Gary didn't want to come ashore here,' Nancy said. 'There's so much to see.' She shook her head. 'I despair of him at times. He doesn't seem to have any pep in him. He should be settled down by now with a family of his own.'

'He seems happy enough,' Hannah said.

'I thought maybe he'd taken a fancy to you, dear, but I can see you're not interested in romance. Not with Gary, anyway.'

Hannah frowned. 'How can you tell?'

Nancy gave her a knowing smile. 'I might be old but I still know romance when I see it.'

'Maybe Tess is the one. They seem to be getting close,' Hannah said, knowing she was prying and hating herself for it.

'You might be right there.' Nancy brightened. 'He could do worse than Tess. She seems a decent sort of woman. Fingers crossed, eh?'

'Now don't you go matchmaking. You'll scare him off.'

'Now, would I ever do that?' Nancy gave a pretend coy look that had Hannah laughing.

But suddenly she felt very possessive of Gary. He'd been there for her over the last few days and it had taken her mind off Nick. Tess had seen how much they had been together. It felt like a betrayal of friendship. She hadn't thought Tess would do that to her.

It made her wonder if it really mattered that she was in danger of losing Gary. Were her feelings for him deeper than she had let herself believe? Was she so obsessed with Nick that she was letting this opportunity slip away from her? And would she live to regret it?

'Penny for them,' Nancy said after they'd sat in silence for a few moments.

'Sorry, I was miles away.'

'Come on, let's get back to the ship and see what they're up to.'

Hannah wasn't sure she really wanted to know. She should have taken her chance with Gary when she'd had it. She felt sure that he had wanted more from her than friendship. And yet she had held him at arm's length.

Slowly she got up and helped Nancy to her feet.

It was a bit of a challenge for Nancy getting back to where the cruise ships were moored, but she soldiered on, and after several stops to get her breath they finally made it back to the Bel Rosa.

'I have so enjoyed today!' Nancy said as they went up the gangway. 'Gary doesn't know what he's missed.'

'You go and have a nice cup of tea,' Hannah suggested. 'Get room service to bring one to your cabin and then you can relax and put your feet up.'

'Ooh, I couldn't do that! I'll just pop down to the coffee bar. The nice girl there made me a lovely cup the other day.'

Hannah shook her head and smiled. There would be no changing Nancy — and who would want to, anyway?

★ ★ ★

Hannah loved standing out on deck in the evening, alone with her thoughts, watching the ship manoeuvre out of the port and pick up speed as it neared the open sea. A yacht sailed into the harbour, its billowing sails tinged golden in the glow of sunset. Astern the lights of Marseille were beginning to twinkle in the early evening light.

Once the ship was out of the harbour she went back to her cabin and flicked through her hangers of dresses for something suitable to wear for the evening. She wasn't hungry yet, so would see what was on in the theatre then eat later.

There was a knock on the door. It was Bryn.

'Have you seen Eleanor?' he asked anxiously.

'Not today, no.'

'I can't find her anywhere.'

Hannah stood aside to let him in.

'Did she go ashore?'

He stalked into the room and turned to face her. 'Yes, I went with her. Didn't want to. But she was fretting about not seeing any of these places. Can't understand the woman. You'd think she'd be content to stay on board. I mean, there's plenty to do. There's a very well equipped library. She tells me she enjoys reading. But she only ever reads those dreadful magazines. Can't understand the woman.'

'Bryn, are you telling me Eleanor's not on board?' Hannah interrupted.

'Well, that's what I'm trying to find out. I'll certainly give her a piece of my mind when I find her. Having me chasing round like this.'

'When did you see her last?' Hannah asked with concern.

'When I left her in that awful shopping mall. Dreadful place. Can't think why she'd want to go round shops when she's got plenty on her doorstep at home. Never could understand women wanting to shop all the time.'

'So you went with her, then left her in a shopping mall?' She was beginning to feel a touch of anxiety.

'That's right. I wasn't going to traipse round shops all afternoon. We'd done a couple of museums. Then we bumped into that Linda woman in the shopping place. Strange woman. Eleanor said she'd like to stay with her. I insisted she come back with me. I told her last night it wasn't a good idea. Not like her to go against my advice. Anyway I agreed in the end and they went off together. I was back on board in time for lunch. Gave me a bit of peace to read the paper without her going on about not doing anything.'

'And you haven't seen her since?'

'Eh, no . . . ' He rubbed his chin.

'Bryn, do you think she could still be ashore, that she hasn't got back to the ship?' Hannah already had her hand on the door handle.

He turned uncertainly to follow her.

'Oh, no, I'm sure she's on board.'

'How are you sure?'

'She told me she was going to have her hair done when she got back. Why she can't do it herself beats me. Thinks I'm made of money. Thought that was where she was. But the salon's closed. I've just been to check up on her. Didn't want her spending money on these fancy treatments. Waste of money, all of them,' he blustered, becoming increasingly red in the face.

147

Hannah raised a hand to stop him.

'Right, we go and find Tess and ask her.'

She almost pushed Bryn out into the alleyway and locked her door. He followed reluctantly, continuing his tirade all the way.

Tess was in her cabin and she wasn't alone. Hannah glimpsed someone sitting on her sofa with a glass of wine. She couldn't be sure but she had a strong feeling it was Gary. But she had more important things to deal with.

'No, she hasn't been in the salon,' Tess said, not asking them in.

'We have to alert security,' Hannah said, taking her phone from her pocket.

'It's that Linda. Should never have agreed to let Eleanor go off with her.'

Hannah stopped him in mid-flow. 'We need to find Linda. See when she last saw her.'

She was beginning to think that if Eleanor had decided to stay in Marseille, she wouldn't blame her. But the poor woman might be ill or in trouble and they had to try to locate her.

Bryn continued ranting as they walked quickly down the alleyway. 'That Linda women has probably filled her head with all sorts of rubbish. I overheard them talking last night out on deck. Didn't hear me coming. Thought I was still in the bar. Has some strange ideas, that woman.'

Hannah took his arm and led him back to his cabin and told him to stay there in case Eleanor turned up. She felt she couldn't cope with much more of his ramblings or she would throttle him! Before leaving him to look for Linda, she tried to calm him but he continued to pace the floor insisting he should be out looking for Eleanor.

'Bryn, I've alerted security. They're doing a systematic search of the ship. Announcements are going out all the time. She's bound to hear one and come back here.'

'She'll have done it on purpose. Done it just to spite me, that's what she's done. Threatened to before. That

Linda will have put it into her head.'

'Don't be silly. She's probably talking to someone out on deck. It's easy to get parted on a ship this size. She might have come back to your cabin while you were in the bar and now she'll be looking for you. We'll find Linda. She'll probably know where she is.'

While trying to reassure Bryn and keep him calm, Hannah was wondering whether there was a grain of truth in what he was saying. Would Linda have talked Eleanor into leaving Bryn? Surely not like this! She had to find Linda fast.

'She's not a well woman, you know.'

'What's wrong with her?' Hannah stopped at the door and turned back abruptly to look at him."

'Suffers from depression. Not easy to live with someone like that.'

Hannah went back in. 'Has she done anything like this before?'

'Threatened to. She's always saying she's going to clear off one day. That she's had enough of me. Never does, though. She knows which side her bread's buttered. Couldn't cope on her own.'

'Has she been treated for depression?' Hannah asked, alarms bells beginning to ring.

Bryn huffed. 'No, I wouldn't have it. It's not an illness, depression. Just needs to pull herself together. That's what I keep telling her. But she doesn't listen. Just goes into one of her silent moods. I leave her to it. She comes round in her own time. Can't be doing with all this malarky.'

Hannah took a deep breath to stop herself screaming at him. 'Bryn, stay here while I go and see what's going on.'

Hannah needed to get away from him before she exploded with exasperation. She also needed to alert someone immediately to this new piece of information about Nancy's depression.

'I'm not staying here doing nothing. My wife is missing. Going to find her and give her a good talking to.' Bryn was pacing the floor becoming more and more agitated.

'Bryn, the whole ship is looking for her. Please stay here. If she turns up and there's no one in your room she'll wander off again.'

He stopped pacing and nodded. 'Sensible idea. You go off then, and tell her I want her back here immediately. Tell her I won't tolerate this sort of behaviour. Never happened in the army. Discipline there. Everyone obeying orders.'

Hannah shook her head in frustration. He was clearly deranged. Maybe Eleanor *had* left him.

She raced down the alleyway to the ship's office and was relieved to find Linda sitting there, stiff-backed, her expression unreadable. After briefing the security officer about what Bryn had told her, Hannah went to sit by Linda.

'I never guessed she'd do anything so stupid,' Linda snapped.

'Do you have any idea where she is?'

Linda shook her head. 'We looked round a few shops and then Eleanor said she'd better get back. I told her not to be silly, that she shouldn't let him rule her life.'

Hannah sighed. 'What was her response?'

'She said she knew that but it had always been that way.' There was a long pause then Linda took a deep breath. 'She said that sometimes she felt like disappearing into the crowd and not having to cope any longer, and I told her that's what she should do. I told her she should get out of it, that a relationship like that wasn't right. Then she wandered off and disappeared into one of the big department stores and I lost sight of her.' She looked at Hannah and winced. 'I think she might have taken my advice rather too literally . . .'

'Linda, you don't know that's what she intended. Don't blame yourself.'

A doubtful expression crossed Linda's face. 'Perhaps not. But I should have kept my mouth shut, shouldn't I?

Minded my own business.' She got up, her brusque manner returning.

'Do you need me here or can I go back to my room?' she asked the security officer.

'Yes, of course you can go.' The woman nodded. 'Thank you for your assistance.'

'I'll come with you,' Hannah offered.

'No!' Linda said abruptly and walked out.

Hannah watched her go and decided she might as well get out of their way as well. She had done all she could. Someone was on their way to take care of Bryn and the search would go on.

She went back to Bryn's cabin. One of the staff was there talking to him and introduced herself as Mel. He was sitting at a window table opposite Mel, his shoulders hunched over and he seemed to have shrunk into himself. Mel was talking to him calmly trying to reassure him that everything possible was being done. Hannah sat quietly and listened to what he was saying and was shocked to see the change in his demeanour. The poor man was in pieces. His brusque manner had completely deserted him.

Mel turned to Hannah and asked, 'Could you sit with him while I find out if there's any news?'

'Of course.' She was happy to help.

Once they were alone Bryn turned to Hannah, concern etched on his face. 'I've not been very kind to her recently. I keep telling her to snap out of it. It's not what she needs to hear, is it?'

Hannah moved to the table where Mel had been sitting so as to sit opposite to him. He cleared his throat and straightened up as if attempting to pull himself together.

'Our daughter keeps telling me I ought to take her to see the doctor, that she needs help. But I wouldn't listen.' His face was full of misery as he turned to stare blankly out of the window. 'Not good at listening. Better at giving orders. Army training, you know.' Then he gave her a despairing look. 'If she's left me, I deserve it.' His face was sagging and all the bluster had gone.

'Let's wait and see what happens. It might not be what you think. She might just have misjudged the time and got left behind. We should hear something soon,' she said gently.

He gave her a resigned look and they sat in silence for some time, Bryn wrapped in his own thoughts, Hannah not feeling there was anything more she could say that would comfort him.

Then the security officer burst into the room, a huge smile on her face.

'It's OK. Eleanor's safe. She got lost and ended up in the local police station. They contacted the cruise company and they're flying her to Palamos so she'll be back on board with you tomorrow when we dock.'

Bryn's face was a picture. First a flicker of uncertainty crossed it, then it transformed into relief, then he was holding back tears. He got up and went to the window to stare out into the distance. Then he turned to them.

156

'Thank you,' he said simply. 'You've both been wonderful. And I'm an old fool. Didn't appreciate what I had until I thought I'd lost it.'

Hannah quietly departed to let them talk about what would happen tomorrow. She went to her cabin with a feeling of satisfaction. At least there would be two happy people on the ship tomorrow.

There was a knock on her door. It was Gary.

'Any news of Eleanor?'

He followed her inside and she filled him in on what had happened.

'What a relief. Poor old Bryn must have been desperate. He's a stuffy old chap but I think his heart's in the right place. I was talking to him down in the bar earlier. He said his wife was ashore shopping, something he couldn't stand.'

'Well, I'm pretty sure he'll go with her next time. He's really fond of her although you'd never think so when you see them together.'

'Anyway, what are you doing for the

rest of the evening?'

'I'm done in, actually. I think I'll grab a bite to eat then come back to my cabin.'

He studied her for a second then smiled.

'OK, no problem. You have a good night's sleep.' Then he was gone.

After eating a burger she'd picked up at the poolside grill, Hannah felt restless. She knew that however tired she was, she wouldn't sleep; she was too wound up. She ran a brush through her hair, grabbed her book and bag and made for the Vista Lounge. There were always people in there relaxing. She might get into conversation with someone, and that would take her mind off the events of the day.

It was a peaceful room, walls a pale terracotta and huge floral arrangements beneath tall elegant lamps. Soft furnishings in cream complemented the colour scheme. Hannah walked over to one of the big picture windows and sank gratefully onto the plush sofa.

She was staring out at the sun as it disappeared below the horizon when she was aware of people standing beside her. She swallowed hard and turned to see it was Gary and Tess.

'So you made it out of your room,' Gary said.

She forced a smile. 'Yes, I couldn't settle after all the drama.'

They sat on the sofa opposite to her. 'You don't mind it we join you, do you?'

'Be my guest,' she said, feeling it was the last thing she wanted.

'I saw Nick earlier. We had a bit of a catch-up on the last few years. I think he's fed up with that Claudia woman chasing after him. He was pretty cut up about the other evening in the abbey when the woman went for you.'

'Yes, it wasn't pleasant,' Hannah mumbled.

'I don't know why she was so angry. I mean, he only went over to talk to you. And why shouldn't he? You've sailed together. It's only natural that he should want to have a catch-up.'

Tess was giving her a concerned look, then she turned to Gary. 'Let's not go over that again. It's best forgotten.'

Gary grunted. 'She's certainly not the sort of person to be working in the salon. When I took Mum down to book a massage, she was really offhand.' He turned to Tess and gave her an affectionate smile. 'But Tess here is going to sort it for her.'

Tess ignored him and gave Hannah a searching look. Hannah quickly turned away, feeling uncomfortable with the situation developing between Tess and Gary.

As if reading her thoughts, Tess got up and said she had a couple of things to do before the morning. This made Hannah feel even worse, thinking Tess had picked up on her feelings.

'Ah, well, Palamos tomorrow. Never been ashore in that port. What have you got planned? Mum wants to look round the town,' Gary said after Tess had left.

'I'll explore the coastline and maybe

take a swim,' Hannah answered mechanically.

'Just the place for it. There are some lovely little coves and beaches. I might have joined you but I don't want Mum going astray and setting off another panic on board.'

'No, we don't want that.' Hannah wished Gary would follow Tess and leave her to her thoughts.

'Anyway, I hope you don't have any more trouble from that crazy woman. Tess says she's jealous of any woman that talks to Nick . . . and here comes the man himself,' Gary exclaimed as Nick approached them.

Nick looked uncomfortable as he hovered, wondering if he should take the seat beside Hannah. She moved to make room for him, feeling that it was the only way to avoid any embarrassment.

He perched on the edge of the sofa, a strained look about him. Gary began to chat to him and Nick answered briefly. Hannah couldn't join in as she was too aware of Nick beside her.

Eventually Gary got up to leave saying he wanted to see if his mum needed anything before she went to bed.

'Better watch out, Nick, or you'll have your lady friend after you again,' Gary joked as he left.

Nick turned to Hannah and for long moments their eyes locked.

'Hannah, she is not my lady friend as Gary so charmingly puts it. And I'm sorry about the other night. Claudia was out of order.'

'You've already apologised. Let's just leave it at that,' she said in a resigned way.

He exhaled softly. Then his eyes narrowed. 'You and Gary seem to be getting on well.'

'Yes, it's been good seeing him again.'

'So, you didn't come together?'

'No, we bumped into each other the first day.'

'And you've been going ashore together?'

'Once or twice.'

'That's good. A ship can be a lonely

162

place when you're on your own.'

'I don't mind. I'm used to it.' She knew she sounded bitter but it was how she felt.

'Well, I'm glad he's looking after you.'

He got to his feet and looked down at her, obviously uncomfortable at the way the conversation was going.

'He's not looking after me. I'm quite capable of looking after myself,' she said, looking up at him defiantly. 'We spend time together because we enjoy each other's company.'

He gave her an exasperated look.

'OK, I get the message.' He closed his eyes for a moment. 'Sorry, I'm making a bad situation worse.'

She watched as he turned and strode away and felt some satisfaction in upsetting him.

8

Hannah woke next morning with an uneasy feeling nagging at her. The way Tess had suddenly gone quiet last night, the look she'd given Hannah when she'd left. She felt sure it had something to do with Gary. Maybe Tess had picked up that Hannah was unhappy about them getting together.

She worried all the way through breakfast until she knew she had to go and see Tess. After finishing her coffee, she marched down to the salon determined to put things right.

In the lift going down she wondered how she could approach the subject and decided to simply ask Tess if she had booked Nancy in for a massage. That would give her the opportunity to detect if there was anything amiss.

Tess was busy blow drying a client's

hair but came to the desk when she saw Hannah.

'I wondered if you'd remembered to book Nancy in for her massage,' Hannah said casually.

Tess gave a gasp. 'Oh, Hannah, I forgot all about it! Good job you reminded me. But yes, of course, I'll see if Pippa's free. Nancy will like her.'

Hannah relaxed. Tess showed no signs that anything was wrong. Perhaps it had all been in her imagination. Reassured, she didn't stay talking as the salon was busy.

The ship was already alongside the quay in Palamos. Hannah lingered on deck a while watching people strolling along a promenade. There was a lovely long stretch of golden sand. Further round the bay were rocky coves. That was where she would head, for a walk along the cliff tops and then a dip in the warm Mediterranean Sea, something she'd promised herself when she'd packed her swimming costume. Then a stroll round the town to see if she could sample some of Palamos's famous prawns.

On the way up to her cabin Bryn caught her.

'Eleanor's on her way up. Will you come with me? I think it might be best.'

He was uneasy, so she was happy to oblige and there was plenty time to go ashore.

Eleanor looked tired and frail as she slowly climbed the gangway, her head bowed. Security checked her pass as she came on board. Bryn watched anxiously. Eleanor saw him standing there, her eyes tearful. He stepped forward and, as she came towards him, he took her in his arms and held her so tight Hannah was afraid he would crush her.

She lifted her face to him. 'I'm so sorry, Bryn,' she sobbed. 'I didn't mean to miss the ship but you know what I'm like.'

'Shush, my dear,' he said crushing her even tighter. 'Yes, I do know what you're like and that's why you need me to look after you.'

'I went into this big shop because I wanted to buy you a present, then I came out in a different street and I couldn't find my way.'

'That was very sweet of you. And did you get me a present?'

She fumbled in her bag but couldn't find what she was looking for and became more flustered.

'Don't worry now. You can give it to me later.'

Her hands were shaking as she finally managed to close her bag and looked up at him.

'They were very kind to me at the police station. They found me a nice little hotel for the night.' Her face creased in anguish. 'I'm afraid you might have to pay the bill. But I can let you have it out of my allowance when we get home.'

Bryn frowned. 'Don't concern yourself with that. You're back safely, all that matters. We'll go back to our room. Get a nice pot of tea sent up. You've had a very distressing experience. You're back now. You're quite safe.'

Hannah backed away discreetly, almost in tears herself as she watched Bryn gently lead his wife through the door from the open deck into the accommodation.

Then she took the lift back to her room. When she stepped out she bumped into Gary.

'I was coming to see you,' he said, looking ill at ease.

As they stood in the open space by the lifts he seemed fidgety, reluctant to begin.

Hannah frowned. 'What's the problem?'

He looked at the floor, then straightened and took a deep breath. 'Hannah, this is difficult . . . '

There was a pause, then she shook her head and smiled at him. 'It's you and Tess, isn't it?'

He nodded, concern etched on his face. 'I don't want to upset you, but . . . '

She put a hand up to stop him. 'Gary, I can see that you and Tess are getting along really well. And I'm pleased for you.'

'No, I knew you would be. But it's Tess. She says that we have to stop going around together. That it will upset you. That you're her friend and she won't do this to you.'

'Do what to me?'

'She thinks that you and I have something going and she doesn't want to intrude.'

Hannah sighed. 'Gary, you've been a good friend to me on this cruise and I appreciate it. But we both know that's all it is.'

'I told Tess that but she won't believe me.'

'Then I'll tell her.' Hannah smiled genuinely.

'Would you do that? She'll have to believe it then,' he said with obvious relief.

Hannah gave him a cheeky smile. 'Are you really getting together? I mean, will you see her after the cruise?'

His face lit up. 'Oh, definitely. We get on so well. She's a lovely lady.' His expression changed. 'I'm not sure she feels the same, though. I don't really know what to think.'

'Well, I'll give her a nudge in the right direction,' Hannah said playfully.

He put his hands up in protest. 'I don't want to push things too quickly. It might put her off.'

'OK, but don't miss out on what might be a fine romance,' she added with a grin. 'You have to let her know how you feel.'

'In my own time,' he said gently but firmly. Then his look softened. 'Thanks, Hannah. And I'm still here for you on this ship if you need me. Tess would never forgive me if I wasn't.'

When he'd gone Hannah felt a warm glow of happiness. Tess was prepared to consider Hannah's feelings before her own. All her resentment evaporated. Tess was a true friend.

With renewed enthusiasm she grabbed her bag and sun hat and was off down the gangway and walking briskly along the quay in the warm sunshine.

After a few minutes she was aware of footsteps hurrying behind her. Thinking it may be someone she knew she turned, then her heart began to thump. Nick was galloping along the quay.

He was panting for breath when he caught up. 'You set a good pace,' he gasped, falling into step alongside her.

'I want to see as much as I can,' she said as she continued to stride along, trying to appear indifferent to his closeness.

'Don't blame you. Where are you heading?'

She refused to look at him. 'I'm going to take a stroll along the coastal path.'

'Mind if I join you?'

'I don't think that's a good idea,' she responded coolly.

'You're worried about Claudia, aren't you?'

'I'm worried about getting involved in your affair,' she snapped.

'Hannah, I keep telling you, there's nothing between me and Claudia.'

'She acts as if there is.'

171

'I know. I admit we were attracted to each other when I first joined the ship. But she's not my type. I realised almost straight away and backed off.'

Hannah shrugged. 'Nick, I'm not interested.'

'Hannah, believe me. Claudia and I are finished. In fact we never really started. Not as far as I'm concerned anyway. I just wish she'd leave me alone.'

'Tell her that. No good telling me.'

'I have told her. I keep telling her. But she won't accept it.'

They walked on in awkward silence for a while then stopped to view a tiny cove beneath the cliff.

Gradually Hannah's heart stopped pounding.

'Can we drop down onto the beach and not talk about Claudia?' she said without looking at him and she heard him release a deep breath.

They took the path down the cliff and found a rocky outcrop to sit on. Soft sand, warm sunshine, the sea gently lapping the rocks and Nick beside her. It should have been perfect, but neither seemed to know how to continue.

Eventually he turned to her. 'I've often thought about you, Hannah, wondered where you where, what you were doing.'

'What I was doing was waiting for you to contact me,' she said bitterly, turning away from him.

'I know, I should have done.'

There was a silence as they both looked down at the sand.

'I just wasn't ready for that sort of commitment,' he said quietly.

'Surely I deserved an explanation. At least I'd have known and not spent weeks wondering.'

'I was afraid you'd talk me into getting a shore job, settling down.'

Her mouth began to tremble and her heart grew tight. 'I wouldn't have done that.'

'No, I don't believe you would,' he said quietly.

He looked out to sea for a moment, then turned back to her. 'I did love you,

Hannah, and I've regretted the way I treated you ever since.'

When he said nothing more she stood up. He followed suit and stood in front of her, his face full of misery. For long moments they stared at each other.

'I'm sorry, Hannah,' he said at last.

She turned her head away from him and, after a few moments of silence, she was aware of him turning and walking away.

The sun was warm on her back yet a shiver of fear ran through her as she watched his slow progress up the cliff. She wanted to stop him leaving, but it was pointless. She had all the answers now. He simply didn't want commitment of any sort — not then, not now. He was a free spirit as Gary had said. Always had been, always would be.

Yet she did have commitments — a young son at home waiting for her to return. She would do well to remember that and not get carried away with silly dreams.

Once at the top Nick looked down and could see her still standing there, a lonely sad figure. Being with her felt more right than anything he had ever known or could have dreamed of. After five years, he still felt the same about her now as he had on that voyage when they had first met. But due to his own selfishness he had let her go. Now, after having seen her again it was hard to contemplate a future without her. Yet he knew in his heart he could never give her what she wanted.

After feeling rooted to the spot for several minutes Hannah wandered further up the beach until she found a sheltered cove. She lowered herself onto the soft warm sand and sat hugging her knees against her chest as she watched the waves lapping the rocks. There was something hypnotic in the rhythm that slowly calmed her.

Eventually she stood and climbed the cliff again, walking with no aim in mind other than to keep going. As she continued along the cliff path, lost in thought, she noticed two figures down on the beach below, one of whom seemed familiar. On closer examination she realised it was Linda and a tall young man, both strolling along the beach barefoot. That was a turn up for the books! Linda had found a man to keep her company. The thought of teasing her about it when she got back on board momentarily cheered her.

Finally she turned back towards the ship. She and Nick had talked. They'd had time together alone. She felt satisfied she now had the answers she had been seeking. She also knew she felt exactly the same about Nick as she had all those years ago. It was an uncomfortable feeling knowing she would never find a love to replace it. So she might as well get used to it.

Zombie-like, she climbed the gangway and went up to her cabin. With the door firmly closed behind her, she flopped face down on the bed, a million thoughts whirring through her head until finally she fell into an exhausted sleep.

An hour later she showered and dressed, determined to put the whole thing behind her. It had been a teenage crush. All those promises of love had meant nothing. He had managed to put her out of his mind and get on with his life. Now she had to do the same. At least something good had come out of it — she had Charlie. Warmth spread through her as she thought about her little boy, at home with her sister, waiting for her return.

Feeling better, she went in search of food. Tess was in the coffee bar and after grabbing a sandwich she went to join her at the table.

'How was your day?' Tess asked, giving Hannah her usual cheerful welcome.

Hannah managed a smile. 'I found a lovely little cove and had a good walk along the cliffs.'

'Good job you were out of the way.'

'Out of the way of what?'

'Madam's been in a fury all afternoon.'

'Claudia?' Hannah sighed inwardly. She did not want to hear any more about Claudia.

Tess finished the doughnut she was eating and wiped the sugar from her lips with a serviette. 'She was planning on taking a couple of hours off to spend with Nick and when she went in search of him she saw him walking along the quay with you. She flew into a rage and she's been shirty with everyone all afternoon.'

'Yes, he did catch up with me. We walked along the cliff path together,' Hannah said defensively.

'Well, good luck explaining that to her.'

Hannah shook her head wearily. 'I have no intention of explaining anything to her.'

Tess gave her a questioning look. 'You've had quite a day with these men, haven't you?'

Hannah felt her colour rise, remembering her conversation with Gary, and she really didn't feel like going through it all again with Tess.

Tess smiled. 'Gary told me he'd been to see you. I told him off. He shouldn't have interfered. And there is nothing between Gary and me so the coast is all clear for you.'

This brought Hannah's mind into quick focus. 'Tess, you've got it all wrong. I knew him from the days on cruise ships. He's a nice guy and as I was alone, he took me under his wing. Nothing more. Please believe me. He's all yours.'

Tess gave an uncertain look. 'Are you sure?'

'Yes, of course I'm sure!' Hannah laughed.

Tess could hardly disguise her pleasure. She jumped up to give Hannah a hug.

'Honestly, I despair of the two of you. I can see how you are together — you're well matched.'

'Well, we have rather clicked . . . '

'So I gather,' Hannah said with a smirk. 'So when do we hear wedding bells?'

Tess blushed. 'Oh, nothing like that.

We have to see how things work out when we get home.'

'Well it couldn't happen to two nicer people.'

'I told Gary he has to keep looking after you.'

'Do you think I need looking after?' Hannah said, relieved the conversation had taken on a lighter tone.

'You know what I mean. You never need to be alone on the ship. We're both here for you. We're all friends, us three, and we'll stick together.' Tess gave her a concerned look. 'I wish it could happen for you,' she said more seriously. 'Claudia thinks you're after Nick, but you're not, are you?'

'Of course not. Whatever gave her that idea?'

'You know what she's like, always reading between the lines. I don't think the attraction is mutual, but Claudia always gets what she wants. Poor Nick doesn't stand a chance.'

'She's not going to last long in her job if she carries on like this,' Hannah said, trying to sound indifferent to what Tess was telling her.

'Don't think she cares. She's made up her mind that she and Nick are going to settle down, then she won't have to work at all.'

'Is Nick thinking of packing in the cruises?' Hannah asked, her insides beginning to churn.

'I don't know about that. Maybe she just wants him to keep her in the style she would like to become accustomed to. I think it's all in her head. She tags onto some poor bloke every cruise. We'd be better off without her. She's a liability.'

Hannah didn't hear any of this as her mind went over what Nick had told her on the beach, how he couldn't contemplate giving up his lifestyle. It was why he had not kept up his relationship with her. Now it appeared he was ready to do just that for this woman. Whatever Tess said, there must be a grain of truth in it. How could she ever trust anything he told her?

'Oh, but you'll never guess who came into the salon earlier,' Tess enthused, changing the subject, for which Hannah was grateful. 'Your friend, Linda. She booked the whole works for later this afternoon. Massage, hairdo, the lot.'

'Wow! I saw her walking on the beach with some bloke earlier. She must really be smitten.'

'Amazing what love can do,' Tess said, getting up from the table saying she was off to her room for a rest. 'I've been at it all day. Didn't even get a lunch break.'

Hannah finished her sandwich then walked back along the alleyway to the lift. Before she reached it Claudia came rushing at her, barring her progress, her face twisted with anger.

'I saw you!' she snarled. 'Walking along the quay together. Very cosy!'

Hannah stood back, startled, but Claudia moved towards her in a threatening manner. 'I don't know what you were up to all afternoon, but you can just keep away from him. Do you hear?'

'I don't know what you're raving about.'

'Oh, you do know what I'm talking about. He told me!' She was shaking with rage. 'He told me he knew you; that you'd sailed together once.'

'Yes, we did. Do you have a problem with that?'

'I have a problem with you two spending the afternoon together.'

'We spoke for a while. That was all. Now please let me past,' she said quietly but firmly.

'He told me you talked about old times.'

'Is that a crime?' Hannah snapped.

'It is when he goes running after you, not even telling me he's going ashore.'

'Is that my fault?'

Claudia made a dismissive noise and turned away, but Hannah saw her face crumple and a faint glitter of tears as her anger subsided.

Not trusting herself to speak again, Hannah squeezed past to continue on her way, still trembling from shock.

9

Hannah sat by the window in her cabin trying to calm herself. The verbal attack from Claudia had sent her reeling and she was terrified of going out of her cabin in case she was confronted again. Yet what she needed was a walk out on deck. So once her heart rate had settled down she ventured along the alleyway determined not to let this jealous woman stop her.

As soon as she went outside she saw Gary and felt more confident; he always made her feel happy and safe, and now she had cleared things with Tess she was comfortable with him again.

She joined him at the ship's rail watching ships manoeuvring in and out of the port.

'Thanks for speaking to Tess, Hannah.' He smiled at her.

'I don't know what all the fuss was about.'

'Neither do I.' He shrugged. 'Anyway it's all sorted now. Are you going to the Cocktails at Sunset party out on deck later?'

'I didn't know there was one. I haven't looked at the programme for today.'

'Well, you'd better get your glad rags on and come along to the pool deck in half an hour when it's supposed to kick off.'

She wasn't in the mood for a party.

'You will come, won't you?' he persisted, giving her a concerned look.

She pulled herself together quickly. 'Of course,' she said with a smile. If she was with Gary and Tess, she would feel safe; Claudia was unlikely to go for her again in front of them.

With a lighter step she did three turns of the deck then went back to her cabin to change.

Eleanor was hovering in the alleyway.

'Oh, I'm so glad I found you,' she said.

Hannah opened her door and stood aside for Eleanor to go in.

'I came earlier but you weren't in your cabin.'

Hannah wondered what was coming.

'I've been ashore all afternoon.'

'Yes, Bryn said you probably would be. You like to get about, don't you?'

'It's what I came for, really, to see all the things I missed when I worked on cruise ships.' There was a pause. 'Is everything all right?' Hannah asked tentatively.

'Oh, yes. I just came to thank you. Bryn said you were very kind yesterday.'

Hannah gave her a reassuring smile.

'We were all worried about you.'

'I know. That's what I wanted to explain. I really did get lost. Bryn said you all thought I'd left him.'

'No, it was Bryn who thought you'd left him.'

Eleanor looked down and fidgeted with the small bag she was clutching. 'I have thought about it. I told him once.' Her chin began to wobble and when she looked up again her eyes were moist. 'He doesn't mean to be unkind. It's his army training, you know. But I never would leave him. I'm not easy to get on with either. He always looks out for me. We understand each other, you know. I really did get lost.'

Hannah smiled. 'You don't have to convince me. You need to tell Bryn.'

'And I have. Everything's fine now. He's been so kind to me since I got back.'

'That's good, then. Maybe it was what he needed. A short sharp shock.'

'That's what he said. But I didn't do it for that.' Eleanor's face lit up in a rare smile and she looked quite beautiful. 'We've been together forty years. I don't see us splitting up now.'

'I don't, either,' Hannah said, feeling a lump forming in her throat.

'I don't want people thinking badly of Bryn because of me,' Eleanor said, frowning again.

'I'm sure nobody will,' Hannah assured her.

'Oh, do you think so?'

'I'm sure of it. Now, you just enjoy the rest of your holiday and don't worry about it.'

'Oh, you've all been so kind,' Eleanor said, dabbing her eyes with a pretty white handkerchief.

Hannah saw her out before she could start all over again and closed the door smiling happily. They were a funny couple but she'd developed quite an affection for them.

★ ★ ★

Half an hour later she was ready to party. Standing in front of the long mirror in her room she smiled. Josie had been right. The long emerald dress set off her newly acquired sun tan and its silky softness draped elegantly over her slim figure. It was perfect for the gala dinner that was to follow the cocktail party on deck. After a final twirl in the mirror she picked up her evening bag, knowing she looked her best.

The pool deck was crowded, the women dressed in evening wear, all with perfect hair and expensive-looking jewellery, the men in dinner suits in honour of the occasion. The ship was slowly making headway towards the open sea leaving churning water in its wake. Groups stood drinking, laughing and chatting. The pool bar was busy serving drinks. A jazz band played on a small stage by the swimming pool. The whole atmosphere was buzzing with chatter and laughter as the sun sank towards the horizon and the sky began to glow a soft vermilion pink.

Hannah hesitated at the edge of the gathering and couldn't see any sign of Tess or Gary. She spotted Linda on her own and went to join her.

'You look great,' Hannah said.

She noticed what lovely clear skin Linda had and, with a touch of make-up and a light wave in her shiny blonde hair, she looked really attractive. The tight-fitting dress she wore just skimmed her knees and showed off her shapely legs. But most of all was the change in her demeanour. There was a softness about her, a sparkle in her eyes and a generally more relaxed manner.

'You don't look so bad yourself,' Linda retorted.

A tall young man in smart dinner suit carrying two wildly decorated cocktails joined them.

'This is Ralph,' Linda said coyly, and Hannah recognised him as the man she had seen Linda walking on the beach with in Palamos.

They shook hands and Hannah thought what an imposing young man he was, just right for Linda, and what a change he'd brought about in her! She positively bubbled with life. Gone was the arrogant air she had assumed before.

After a brief conversation Hannah saw Gary, and he and Tess beckoned to her.

'I think your friends over there want you to join them,' Linda said.

'Are you trying to get rid of me?' Hannah joked.

Linda blushed, a sight Hannah had never thought to see. She excused herself and went to join Tess and Gary.

'We were wondering where you were,'

Tess said, giving her a hug.

'Just talking to Linda. That young man she's teamed up with seems very nice.'

'Ah, so now we know the reason for the makeover,' Tess said with a knowing smile.

Gary gave her a questioning look but she just put a finger to her lips and he raised an eyebrow.

'Well, you're here now,' he said to Hannah, placing a cocktail in her hand.

'Cocktails at Sunset. That's what the programme said. And we have live music.'

'And then a gala dinner,' Hannah added, hoping they would invite her to join them. She didn't fancy eating alone.

Gary must have been reading her thoughts. 'You must sit with us. That's unless you've made other arrangements.'

'I'd love to,' she said.

'Mum's around somewhere. We'll find her before we go in.'

So the 'us' meant him and Nancy. Hannah couldn't help a feeling of relief; it would be much easier than playing gooseberry to a couple.

'Tess can't join us unfortunately. It's just for the passengers,' Gary said, clarifying the matter.

'Can't wait to get my feet up,' Tess said.

Hannah gave her a sympathetic smile. 'I know that feeling. Perhaps we'll see you later.'

'Oh, I'm sure I'll get my second wind eventually.' She winked at Gary.

Again Hannah felt a surge of longing. Everyone seemed to be sorting out their relationships except her. Until she'd stepped on this ship she'd been content with her life, happy to be with Charlie and Josie. Any thoughts of romance had left her long ago. But now, surrounded by couples, she had begun to yearn for someone special in her life — yet she knew in her heart it could only be Nick. And that was never going to happen.

The sky was ablaze with colour, the sea tinged golden. Hannah sipped her cocktail and surveyed the scene as Gary and Tess talked quietly beside her. This was what she had come on the cruise for and she was determined that nothing was going to spoil her last evening on board. Once she was off this ship tomorrow and away from it all she'd be OK again. After her week in Barcelona she'd go home and settle down and stop acting like a lovesick schoolgirl. For the time being, she just wanted to enjoy the rest of her holiday.

She turned to join in the conversation with Tess and Gary, not wanting them to think she was being unsociable. As she did so she spotted Nick on the opposite side of the deck, leaning on the rail staring out to sea, with Claudia beside him. Despite her best intentions, her heart began pounding. She hadn't expected to see him at this gathering as she supposed he would be in the galley making sure the gala dinner lived up to expectations. And she certainly didn't want another confrontation with Claudia.

Nick turned and their eyes met. He smiled, an uncertain one, full of doubt.

It seemed an age before he looked away and Hannah had never felt more vulnerable.

After long moments she managed to join in the conversation with Gary and Tess, but she couldn't help a sideways glance in Nick's direction every now and again. He turned to Claudia and said something but didn't smile. She seemed to snap back. Then he turned away from her and Claudia gave him a sour look and stalked off along the deck towards the accommodation.

'Are we going in to dinner, then?' Gary broke into her thoughts.

Hannah quickly pulled herself together. Tess had disappeared and Gary was alone beside her.

'Where's Tess gone?' she asked, surprised she hadn't noticed her leave.

'Oh, she did say cheerio to you but you seemed in a daydream so she just laughed and went off to relax in her room while we dine. But it was nice she managed a drink with us.'

'Oh,' Hannah said again. 'I was

watching the sunset. It's so beautiful.'
Then she realised she had been looking
in the opposite direction. Gary just
smiled and shook his head and Hannah
felt so silly. She really did have to get a
grip.

'Look, I have to find Tess to give her
this. She's left it behind.' Gary was
holding a jacket Tess had slung over the
back of a chair.

Hannah didn't offer to take it. She
simply wasn't thinking straight.

'I'll be back in a minute then we can
find Mum and go into dinner together,'
he told her.

Hannah nodded, grateful that Nancy
would be there to bring her down to
earth.

As soon as Gary had gone she felt a
tap on her shoulder and turned. Nick
stood there, handsome in his uniform
white shirt, his smooth tanned face
dark against those pale blue eyes.

'Are you going into the gala dinner?'
he asked.

Her heart began thumping once

again as his nearness both disturbed and excited her. 'Yes, I'm just waiting for Gary.'

'That's OK then. I didn't want you sitting on your own.' He stood uncertainly as she looked up at him. 'I could have found you a table with some friendly people.'

She looked away, trying to gain some sort of control. 'Thank you. But I'm fine.'

'I just saw you standing there alone . . . '

The music, the sunset, the whole atmosphere on deck was so romantic.

He turned as if to go.

'Nick, stop,' she called after him.

He gave a surprised look, then moved back towards her. She quickly looked out over the sea, embarrassed at her own involuntary action. They stood side by side at the ship's rail.

Now she had to think of something to say. Anything to keep him beside her.

'Claudia didn't seem happy about you following me ashore today,' she said, not able to come up with anything else. Her brain seemed to have gone numb.

He gave a great sigh. 'Claudia is a problem.'

'I agree with that,' she said with feeling.

'I've had all I can take from her. I've tried to shrug her off, let her know in a nice way that I'm not interested, but she won't take the hint. She can't believe there's a man who doesn't succumb to her charms.'

'So, what will you do?'

He hunched his shoulders. 'I don't want to be unkind but I'm beginning to think some strong talking is the only thing that will get through.'

They fell silent again.

Then he turned to her. 'I felt unhappy the way we parted on the beach today. I know I let you down. I deserve all your anger, but can't we part on good terms? It would be nice if we could go our separate ways with fond memories rather than bad ones.'

There was so much pain in her heart she could hardly bear it. She wanted to be with him. She wanted him to take her in his arms and hold her and tell her everything was going to be all right, that he loved her and he wanted them to be together for ever. But he wasn't saying that.

He moved in front of her and took both her hands in his. 'One dance,' he said quietly. 'Something good to remember.'

She followed as he led her to the almost deserted dance floor where the musicians were still playing, then enfolded her in his arms.

She knew she should have pulled away but he'd told her that Claudia meant nothing to him and from what she'd seen, she was beginning to believe him. She wanted so much to believe him. So why shouldn't she steal a few moments of happiness with the man she loved?

As they began to move to the music Hannah knew it was where she belonged, where she had belonged when they had first met. It all came rushing back to her as if the intervening five years had never been. They were the arms that had made her feel safe, the arms that had taken away all the homesickness and in its place put love and happiness.

The musicians were playing a Nat King Cole song, *Unforgettable*, as they moved round on that small dance floor below a pale twilight sky with the twinkle of fairy lights dappling the deck beneath them.

'*Unforgettable, that's what you are,*' Nick murmured as he pulled her closer, his voice low with emotion. Warmth spread through her as she leaned into him and all she wanted was to savour this moment with this man and let the rest take care of itself.

The dance ended, but he didn't release her, seemed lost in thought, then slowly he slipped a hand round her neck, leaned in and kissed her. It was unbearably tender, filled with unspoken longing. And in that moment she was lost.

'I've been wanting to do that since I saw you come on board,' he said, staring down at her.

As they stepped apart he held her gaze and the air between them was heavy with emotion. She stood a moment mesmerised by those blue eyes, unable to think straight.

When she did turn away, a cold chill made her skin prickle — Claudia was bearing down on them and the look on her face spelled trouble!

The next few minutes were a haze. Claudia pushed between them, her features contorted with ugly rage. Hannah lost her balance and would have fallen backwards onto the deck if Gary had not steadied her. Nick took a firm hold of Claudia's arms and pulled her away. There was a lot of shouting. The few people left on deck were gathering round. Gary led Hannah to the side of the ship and found a chair for her to sit on.

'Are you all right?' Gary asked.

'Yes,' she gulped, trying to stop shaking.

'That woman is mad! They should take her off the ship. It's the second time she's caused a scene,' Gary said. 'Look, Mum's here.'

Nancy rushed to Hannah, concern etched on her face. 'What happened? I heard the rumpus.'

'It's OK,' Hannah managed as she straightened her dress and tried to smile.

'Do you want to go back to your room, dear?'

'No, let's go in to dinner,' she gasped in a shaky voice.

Gary looked uncertain, but Nancy agreed it was the best thing to do. 'We'll get you a nice brandy to calm your nerves,' she told Hannah, taking her arm.

Gary looked stunned but followed the two women towards the lifts.

Inside the restaurant the quiet ambience calmed Hannah. The large brandy Nancy insisted she drank soon had her relaxed again. Neither Nancy nor Gary questioned why Claudia had gone for her. Hannah suspected they had seen her with Nick and would have put two and two together but she was beyond caring what anyone thought.

The room had been specially prepared for this dinner with place cards for each of the guests and large, gold-rimmed menus of the courses they would be served. A fountain gurgled gently amid beautiful floral arrangements on a central dais and a harpist in a long flowing gown played classical music on a small stage.

Hannah stared at the single red rose at the centre of the table and picked up the pretty sachet of pot-pourri that lay in front of her and inhaled its delicate perfume.

The food began to arrive, course after course of gourmet dishes, artistically arranged on the plates. Hannah was just thankful the portions were so small. She was grateful that she was safely seated at a table with Gary and Nancy where she did not feel compelled to take part in any serious conversation, although she managed to find the words to answer their questions.

★　★　★

After the gala dinner had finished, Tess caught up with them as they came out.

'I hear Madam's been at it again,' she said. 'Are you all right, Hannah?'

Hannah looked sheepish, realising that by now Tess would have worked out what was going on.

'Yes, I'm OK. Just shocked,' she said, feeling guilt running through her. She didn't want to discuss any of it with anyone. What she really wanted was to forget it had even happened, get off this ship and go home.

'Well, I hope someone makes sure she doesn't do anything like it again,' Nancy said with feeling.

'I don't think there's much chance of that. I bet she's in her room now, repenting,' Tess said.

'What are we going to do now, then?' Gary asked, looking to Tess. 'I think we ought to party down in the Hub. Try and forget this happened.'

'I'm game,' Tess said.

'How about you, Hannah? End the evening with a bit of dancing, get you back on track again.'

'No, I think I'll retire for the night.' She couldn't bring herself to join them in the Hub after what had happened.

'Are you sure you're all right?' Tess said.

'I'm fine. Just tired.'

'OK, but if you change your mind you know where we are.'

'And if that one bothers you again, you come and get me,' Nancy put in.

'I'll see you ladies in the morning then,' Gary said cheerfully, taking Tess's arm.

After they left her Hannah didn't go back to her room immediately but wandered along the deck. The shock of Claudia was fading into oblivion and all she could think of was being in Nick's arms again, and how it had felt.

Once in her cabin she turned on the radio. Lying there in the dark she listened to the haunting melody of *Love Is In The Air*.

Nick would find Claudia and they would make up their quarrel. Tess and Gary would be dancing in the Hub. And she was alone in her room.

A terrible loneliness engulfed her and she buried her head in the pillow and sobbed.

10

After she had cried out all the pain, Hannah decided the night was still young and she was not going to sit in her cabin and mope. It was the end of the cruise, after all, and there would be partying all over the ship and she was determined her last night on board would be a good one. She didn't care who saw her or what they would think. Nobody, not even Claudia would stop her. Tomorrow she'd be off this ship and would never see any of them again.

As soon as she got inside the Skylight bar she saw Claudia sitting on her own at one of the small tables with a large glass of wine in front of her. There was no sign of Nick. Hannah made her way cautiously towards the central bar. If Claudia caused another scene there were plenty of people around to deal with it. All she had to do was keep her head and not react.

Once she was seated on a bar stool, she felt more comfortable. The barman was friendly and chatted to her while he poured her drink. When he moved on to his next customer she glanced in Claudia's direction and was relieved to see she had gone. An older couple at the bar began to chat to her and as the drink relaxed her, she felt her mood lighten.

She was about to get up and find out what was going on in the rest of the ship when Tess and Gary came in and joined her.

'I thought you were retiring for the evening and here you are boozing!' Tess said, laughing.

'That really was my intention, but then I got my second wind.'

'You should have been in the Hub just now. Gary had an offer he couldn't refuse,' Tess said, giving Gary a cheeky smile. He looked embarrassed.

'Oh, tell me!' Hannah said.

'We were just about to leave when

Claudia appeared. She made for the dance floor and draped herself around some poor unsuspecting bloke. We were having a good laugh at her. Then he broke free and she looked round and spotted us. Next thing she's staggering over and grabbed Gary!' Tess could hardly continue for laughing.

Hannah tensed, not comfortable with the conversation returning to Claudia. Gary was looking uncomfortable too.

'I tried to get rid of her. But she clung on.'

'Are you sure you weren't temped?' Tess was enjoying teasing him.

'Behave yourself, woman!' Gary admonished. 'I tried to disentangle myself but she wasn't having any of it. I let her drag me onto the floor.'

'Poor old Gary was well and truly lumbered,' Tess said.

'I didn't want any more trouble. I thought if I humoured her she'd go away.'

'It was so comical. Poor old Gary was out of his depth. He did manage to escape eventually and left her in the middle of the floor. She was so far gone I don't think she even noticed.'

'She's like a leech, that one. I feel sorry for Nick. He doesn't seem able to disentangle himself from her either.'

'He's too nice, that's his problem,' Tess muttered. 'He should be firm and just tell her to get lost!'

'I don't see why she had a go at you, though,' Gary said, turning to Hannah.

'Oh, she's paranoid. Thinks every woman who talks to Nick is after him,' Tess said airily.

'But Hannah knows him. Why should they ignore each other just to please Claudia?'

'I agree.' Tess said with a shrug.

'So where is she now?' Hannah asked, relieved that the other two had not realised what had led up to Claudia's behaviour.

'Still dancing as far as I know. She'll tag onto some other poor bloke. Can't think how she's managed to keep her job for so long,' Gary said, looking towards Tess.

'She's good when she's sober. She certainly transformed Linda when she did her make-up for the gala dinner.'

'Let's hope she finds her bed and doesn't go for a swim.'

Hannah started in alarm, then realised Gary was joking.

'Do you think they'll have her back?' Hannah asked tentatively.

'Not if you complain about what happened on deck. Then they'd have to investigate,' Gary said.

She shook her head. 'I wouldn't do that. She didn't do me any real harm and I wouldn't want to be responsible for her losing her job.'

Tess sighed. 'I think she'll do that all by herself. I don't blame you keeping out of it, though.'

Hannah nodded as a stab of guilt shot through her. She knew she should not have been dancing with Nick while Claudia was around. It had been asking for trouble.

'And guess who we saw on the dance floor?' Tess said, breaking into her thoughts. 'Linda was with Ralph and they were dancing very close.'

'Looks like Linda's had a change of heart,' Hannah said. 'I saw them earlier and Linda seemed like a changed woman.'

'If it can happen to Linda, it can happen to anyone.' Tess gave Gary a coy look.

'Anyway, what we came to ask you was if you fancied coming down to the Dance The Night Away party out on deck. It's in full swing now. We're going if you want to join us.'

'I'd love to.' A warm glow of happiness lifted Hannah's spirits.

Gary sighed. 'It's the last night and I haven't even started packing for home yet.'

Tess nudged him playfully. 'Your mum will have done that for you!'

* * *

The party on deck was noisy with music and chatter as they merged into

211

the crowd. Hannah caught sight of Linda walking off the dance floor with Ralph, then he left her standing on her own.

'I'll just go and have a word with Linda,' she told Tess. 'I might not see her tomorrow and I would like to say cheerio.'

'Looks like you got yourself a fella,' Hannah teased, feeling light-hearted now that the incident with Claudia seemed to have passed.

Linda looked rather embarrassed.

'Oh, we were just dancing.'

'I thought how nice he was when we met on deck before.'

'He's OK, but don't start putting two and two together. I'm allowed a dance, aren't I?'

'Well, of course but I thought you two were together . . . I saw you on the beach earlier and you looked pretty cosy to me.'

Linda straightened to her full height. 'Well, he's a nice bloke . . . '

'I thought you were of the opinion

there weren't any of those in existence,' Hannah teased.

'Well, maybe there are. I just haven't come across one.'

'Until today.'

'Actually, we met on the first day of the cruise.'

'And you didn't let on?' Hannah exclaimed.

'I had to be sure.'

'And are you sure now?'

'Yes, absolutely! He's a real gentleman.'

'Well, here's your gentleman coming back with drinks for you.'

Ralph's smile was warm and he had an intellectual air about him that would suit Linda.

'Wait until I tell Tess!' she whispered to Linda when Ralph was distracted with a couple trying to get past them onto the dance floor.

Linda tried to look stern but then nudged her and winked happily.

★ ★ ★

It was much later, when most of the party-goers had drifted back to their rooms, that Hannah sat watching a couple circle the dance floor holding each other in a close embrace.

The deck was bathed in moonlight, almost deserted now. The musicians by the pool played on. A small group of passengers lingered, their buzz of conversation drifting through the air.

The deck bar was closing down, the barman polishing glasses. It had been a perfect last evening on board. Gary had danced with her. Tess had been in party mood and they had laughed and joked together. Linda and Ralph had joined them for a while. The drinks had flowed.

Now Hannah was alone.

Tess had worried about leaving her but she'd insisted she wanted to spend some time by herself before turning in. It was peaceful sitting in the cool evening air with the sound of the sea and the gentle night music.

Tomorrow she would leave all this behind. Tonight she wanted to savour every moment. Some good memories to sustain her in the difficult days ahead.

The barman was beginning to give her concerned looks. She knew she'd drunk too much. She knew she ought to get up and move inside. But still she sat, a lone, sad figure reluctant to go to a solitary bed.

She stared mutely into her empty glass. She didn't want to move. She didn't want to finish her packing. She didn't want to face the future. Sitting out on deck, she knew he was close by. Somewhere on this ship was the man she loved. Would he be thinking of her? She could almost feel his presence.

She knew she couldn't stay out on deck much longer. It was well past midnight. If she didn't move soon someone was sure to come and ask if she was all right.

Trying to get to her feet she stumbled, and in doing so caused the chair to tip over making a clatter. Mortified that she was going to end up sprawled on the deck in an undignified manner she clutched at the table. It rocked unsteadily.

Then strong arms steadied her and she turned to see Nick shaking his head in amusement as his kind eyes smiled into hers.

Once she had gained her composure he took her elbow and steered her over to a table nearer the side of the ship, out of the lights of the bar.

'Do you mind if I sit with you a while?'

'So long as your mad girlfriend doesn't come at me again,' she managed without slurring her words too much.

'She won't,' he said, taking a seat opposite to her. 'And she's not my girlfriend. Never has been, never will be.'

The barman brought a glass of beer out to Nick and asked if Hannah wanted anything.

'Just a glass of water,' Nick answered for her. 'So you're off home tomorrow?' he said lightly.

'Not quite. I'm staying in Barcelona for a week.' She tried to smile but her face was tight.

'Ah, yes, that's an option, isn't it? You'll like it, I can promise you.'

They were silent for a while as they stared out over the ocean into the dark night.

Hannah swallowed hard to stay in control but could feel the tears gathering. He noticed.

'You weren't in your cabin so I came looking for you. I wanted to check you were all right after what happened before on deck.'

'She saw us together. We shouldn't have been. She was angry,' Hannah stuttered.

'But she has no right to be. She must realise by now that I'm not interested in her.'

'It seems like more than that to me.'

'Hannah, I'm telling you it's not. In fact I told her firmly this afternoon to leave me alone. That's why she's so angry.'

'Did it have anything to do with us getting together in Palamos?' she asked.

'I have no idea what goes on in her mind. This is the third trip I've been on the same ship with her. She just won't let go and I've had enough.'

'So where does that leave us?'

She could hardly believe she'd said it. The words had slipped out. It must have been the wine. She wasn't used to drinking so much.

She could see he was taken aback by her boldness.

After a brief pause he shook his head slowly.

'Hannah, I can't form a relationship even if I wanted to. Not with Claudia, not with you, not with anyone. This life doesn't make it possible. You know that, Hannah.'

She stared at him thinking anything should be possible if he loved her.

'But there must come a time when you'll want to settle down,' she ventured.

He shook his head. 'I don't think there will be. I love this life too much. Different ships. Different places. Different people. I'd get bored working in one place.'

She nodded slowly and choked back

the tears. He still wanted to be free to go wherever life took him. He always had and he always would.

She stood up in an attempt to leave but as she did so he was quickly by her side, put an arm round her waist and guided her over to the rail where they stood together beneath the black velvet sky.

Water gently lapped the sides of the ship as it drew ever nearer to their final port where they must say goodbye for ever. Tomorrow she would leave the ship and knew now that she would never see Nick again.

The clear soft voice of a woman singing *Somewhere Over The Rainbow* came floating across the deck. Her head began to clear in the cool night air and she looked up at Nick. As their eyes met they were both remembering how they had danced out on deck to that song once before.

'Hannah, I wish it could be different,' he murmured, a sadness creeping over his face.

As they looked into each other's eyes, his arm still round her waist, she felt the closeness they had shared when they had first met. A shaft of moonlight lit up his face and she could see passion contorting his features.

Then his arms encircled her and he gazed down at her with eyes full of love. She rested against him, his warmth making her feel safe as it had done once before when she had felt so unhappy and alone. He pulled her close and his lips touched hers. His kiss was unbearably tender, filled with unspoken longing, and her whole being ached for this man whom she had held in her heart for so long.

When he released her he took both her hands in his and squeezed them gently.

'I won't ever forget you,' he whispered, his clipped voice telling her how emotional he was.

The musicians were playing the last waltz.

'One lasting memory,' he whispered.

She hesitated but was helpless under his power. He gripped her hand tightly and led her to the poolside and she was in his arms again, a lone couple, on that small square of deck in front of the musicians as they played and she let the beauty of the night and the music fill her heart.

All too soon the music stopped.

Nick looked down at her and seemed to be lost in thought, then slowly and very gently he leaned in and kissed her. He held her close for a last embrace and then let her go.

She stood and watched as he disappeared into the night, aching with longing. So that was it. Memories were all they would ever have now.

It was Tess who appeared by her side and took her arm and led her back to her cabin. She gave her a hug and made sure she was safely inside before she left her.

Zombie-like she undressed and crept into bed. Lying in the dark she relived every moment of that dance; the feel of his arms around her chasing away her heartache.

She knew he still loved her. Yet he had walked away and left her.

Her radio was tuned into late night music and she drifted into sleep with Frank Sinatra crooning *'What now my love, now that you've left me?'* It seemed the words were meant for her but there were no answers. Soon he would be gone and she would be alone again.

11

Hannah woke next morning just as dawn was breaking, her head buzzing with a million thoughts. Unable to get back to sleep, she wandered out onto the deck. Ominous black clouds were forming on the horizon, tinged orange by the rising sun, and a feeling of dread consumed her.

Tess caught up with her at breakfast.

'Ready for the off, then?' she asked.

'Yes, I'm almost packed.'

'You're staying in Barcelona for a week, aren't you, before you fly home?'

'That's the plan,' Hannah said. She just couldn't dispel the gloom that encompassed her this morning.

'At least you won't have Claudia to worry about,' Tess said as they stood in line for food.

'No, thank goodness. She's the one person I hope never to see again.'

'Lucky you. I'm stuck with her for another cruise — and Nick's in trouble again.'

'What's he done now?' Hannah really didn't care, but she did wonder how much of the situation Tess had picked up on, whether she had guessed what was going on.

'He's only gone and asked for shore leave in Barcelona, and Madam's livid! She thought he was staying on board for the next cruise.' Tess chuckled. 'I can't imagine why he would want to do that, but he probably thinks it's the only way he can escape from her.'

This brought Hannah up with a jolt and she nearly dropped the tray she was carrying.

Nick was leaving the ship in Barcelona at the same time as she was!

They found a table and Hannah couldn't stop her hands shaking as they unloaded their food.

Tess chattered on. 'Nick probably thought if he left it to the last minute to tell her she wouldn't be able to follow him. Once he's on that plane he's safe from her.'

Of course. He'd be flying back home to England. A confusion of relief and disappointment ran though Hannah. Her head was all over the place!

Tess was still going on. 'I don't know why he hasn't put her straight long ago, but he's too gentlemanly, that's Nick's problem. I told her she should ask for leave too, keep him company, but that didn't go down too well.' Tess couldn't conceal her amusement. 'Evidently she'd suggested it and he told her in no uncertain terms that he didn't want her hanging around him any more. About time too! No good mincing your words with that one.'

When Hannah didn't respond Tess put her knife down and gazed at her steadily.

'You've gone very quiet. Is there something I'm missing here?'

Hannah stared miserably across the table at her trying desperately to hold back the tears.

'It's Nick, isn't it?'

Hannah looked away.

'Oh, Hannah, I'm sorry. Me and my big mouth!'

'I thought you might have guessed.'

'No, it was the way you went silent just then. So that's why Claudia's been acting up, ranting on about how you've stolen him from her. And the way she went for you last night! I thought it was all in her mind. She gets these obsessions. What's really going on, Hannah?'

Hannah took a deep breath. 'When Nick and I sailed together we got very close. I wasn't expecting him to be on this ship, and it's sort of brought the whole thing back.'

'How long ago was that?'

'Five years.'

'It must have been a shock for you.'

'Yes, it was. I hoped we wouldn't come into contact with each other, especially when I knew he was with Claudia. But somehow it seems like it was inevitable.'

'I had no idea. How long were you together?'

'Only that one cruise.'

'And you didn't see him afterwards?'

'No, he went on leave and I stayed on the ship. We never sailed together again.'

'Didn't you keep in touch at all?'

'I tried to, but he just cut me off completely.'

Tess looked puzzled. 'That doesn't sound like Nick to me. He always struck me as a decent bloke. And he's been really patient with Claudia, especially when you think how badly she's treated him. Most men would have told her to clear off long ago.'

'Well, he obviously thinks more of her than he did of me. I phoned him and sent texts and emails and he never answered even one.'

Tess frowned. 'There must have been a reason, Hannah.'

'I spoke to him about it. He said he couldn't see how it would work out with both of us on different cruises.'

Tess sighed. 'He was probably right. It's why I've never managed to sustain a relationship.'

'But why didn't he talk to me about it at the time?' Hannah countered.

'Probably thought you'd try and persuade him to give up the cruises and get another job.'

Hannah looked down at her untouched food. 'That's exactly what he said. But I wouldn't have done that.'

'Nick didn't know that, though, and you'd only spent a few weeks together. Do you still have feelings for him, Hannah . . . ?'

'I always have,' she said in a small voice.

'And does he feel the same?'

'I think he might. He *has* been following me round the ship. Whenever I'm out on deck he seems to pop up and want to talk to me.'

'And that's why Claudia went for you yesterday evening?'

'Well, we were dancing together . . . '

Tess winced. 'Oh dear . . . it's all

starting to make sense now. Why didn't you tell me? Talking about it might have helped.'

'I suppose I was in denial, Tess, trying to pretend it didn't matter. It was years ago. I should be over it by now.'

'But you're obviously not.' A heaviness hung in the air. 'So what now?' Tess said gently.

'Nothing. We talked last night. He still doesn't want to be tied down.'

'Men! Honestly! I'm glad I'm still single.'

Hannah felt herself slump. Talking to Tess had given her some relief but it didn't offer any solutions and the pain was still the same.

Tess looked distraught. 'I'm so sorry. I wish there was something I could do to help.'

Hannah gave a resigned smile. 'You have helped, Tess. I don't know how I would have coped without you and Gary on this cruise. I just have to get over it. I'm determined to put it all behind me once I'm off the ship.'

'At least he's going home so you won't be in danger of bumping into him again. And you'll be at home with your sister.'

'And Charlie.' She closed her eyes and winced. It had just slipped out.

'Who's Charlie?'

'He's my son . . . '

It was actually a relief to tell someone and Tess didn't gossip.

Tess gasped. 'You have a son? You never mentioned that!'

'I didn't want it to get back to Nick.'

There was a stunned silence as Hannah looked down at her plate. Eventually she found her voice.

'Charlie is Nick's son . . . '

Tess stared at her, stunned. 'And Nick doesn't know? Oh, Hannah!'

Hannah shook her head. 'I don't want him to know. He wouldn't want to get involved. He values his freedom too much. If he can't even sustain a relationship, how could he take on a child?'

'I can't believe what you're telling me!'

'Please don't say anything. No one

230

on board knows, and I don't want it to get back to Nick.'

'Of course not,' Tess assured her. 'So where is Charlie now?'

'My sister's looking after him. We manage between us.'

Tess stared at her in shocked silence. 'Hannah, I don't know what to say.'

Hannah managed a watery smile. 'Let's talk about you and Gary. You will keep in touch with him, won't you?'

It brought a smile to Tess's face. 'Yes, we're meeting up as soon as I get home on leave.'

'That's great, Tess.'

'We get on so well together, and he doesn't live far from me. To tell the truth I'm thinking of doing what you've done. It wouldn't be difficult to get a hairdressing job back home.'

'Wow, it must be love!'

Tess sighed. 'It would be nice to have someone special. I don't want to grow old and lonely.' She put a hand over her mouth. 'I've gone and put my foot in it again. I shouldn't have said that.'

'Don't be silly. I'm happy for both of you.'

'That's great but don't start hearing wedding bells just yet,' Tess said, raising an eyebrow.

'Tess, if he's the one, don't put it off. Take all the happiness you can. You're right, it can be lonely on your own.'

'I know. I've been there. I was in love once but it didn't work out. Most blokes won't wait for a girl who's away on cruise ships for months on end. But I loved the job more than the man at that time.'

'Then don't let it happen again. Take this chance while you've got it. There aren't many like Gary around.'

'You're right there. We'll see . . . '

Hannah felt a lump forming in her throat and Tess noticed.

'Hannah, I'm so sorry. I don't know what else to say. I hope you find someone eventually. After all, look at me — I never guessed it would happen on this cruise.'

Hannah gave her a wistful smile. 'I

hope it works out for you, Tess, I really do.'

'I have to leave now,' Tess said, getting up. 'Got to wind up in the salon before we dock.'

They gave each other a hug and promised to keep in touch.

Hannah finished her coffee then set off back to her cabin to complete her packing. Tess said she hoped she'd find someone eventually but she knew she wouldn't. Nobody could ever replace Nick in her heart. And nothing anyone could say would make her feel any better.

She bumped into Nancy on her way out of the restaurant.

'Oh, there you are, dear. I was looking for you.'

'And I was on my way to find you,' Hannah said with forced cheerfulness.

'You're staying on in Barcelona, aren't you?' Nancy said.

'Yes, that's right. And you're going straight home, I gather?'

'We are. Gary has to get back to work

on Monday, and I'm ready for home. It's been a lovely holiday but I'll be glad to get back to my little house again.'

They chatted as they walked to the lift and while they were waiting for it to come Nancy turned to Hannah, a serious look on her face. She patted her arm. 'Now you look after yourself and don't you let love slip by.'

'Nancy, Gary's a lovely person and I've enjoyed being with him this week, but it's not what you think. Gary and I are just friends.'

'Oh, I don't mean my Gary. He's much too old for you and I think he's a bit sweet on Tess. No, dear, I mean Nick . . . and don't even try to tell me he's just a friend.'

Hannah sighed. You couldn't keep much from Nancy. She was so perceptive.

'We sailed together years ago.'

'And now he's back in your life.'

'No, not really.'

Nancy gave her a quizzical look. 'It's not what I've heard.'

'What have you heard?'

'Well, I went into the coffee bar yesterday to say goodbye to that nice lady who used to serve me and to thank her for being so kind to me. There were some other people there and they were all talking about Claudia and I couldn't help hearing your name crop up. And I thought how nice it would be if you and Nick got together instead of him being stuck with that awful woman.'

While Nancy prattled on Hannah was trying to process all this. She had no idea the whole ship was talking about her and Nick!

That would be down to Claudia. She would have been spreading malicious rumours as she worked on her clients in the treatment room. She wasn't going to go away quietly. That wasn't Claudia's style. It was surprising Tess hadn't picked up on it.

Nancy was still chattering on. 'And I saw you out on deck last night. I only went out for a breath of fresh air because I couldn't sleep. And there the two of you were staring into each other's eyes and I thought you made such a lovely couple.'

Finally Nancy stopped and they both looked round as Claudia passed them hand in hand with one of the waiters. Claudia gave them a smug look and passed on.

Nancy tutted. 'Well, it doesn't look as if she's broken-hearted!'

Hannah shook her head. 'Nancy, Nick and I are not getting together.'

Nancy sighed. 'What a shame. Ah, well, I suppose I can't fix everything!'

The lift arrived and Gary stepped out. They let it go up again so they could say their farewells. Gary gave her a hug and told her to take care. When the lift reappeared they all got in.

★　★　★

The one person she did not want to say goodbye to was Nick. It would be too painful and she hoped she wouldn't bump into him. The memory of that last time when she had watched him walk down the gangway with his rucksack slung over his shoulder was fixed in her mind. The look he had given her as he briefly turned had stayed with her all these years. The way her heart had clenched. A lasting memory to haunt her.

All Hannah wanted now was to get off the ship and to her hotel where nobody would know her and she could try to sort out her troubled mind. In fact, what she really wanted was to go home and be with Charlie again. Talking about him had stirred up her emotions and she longed to have her little boy in her arms.

She finished her last-minute packing in a calmer mood and was ready to disembark when the ship docked. After closing her suitcase, she put it in the alleyway for the porters to collect then decided she would go and sit in the Vista Lounge where she could relax and watch the ship approach the port.

As she came out through her cabin

door for the last time, Claudia appeared and barred her way.

Hannah let out a long moan. 'What now?'

Claudia stood in front of her, an ugly sneer distorting her face. 'So you've got what you wanted!' she spat out.

Hannah shook her head wearily. 'I don't know what you're talking about. Please let me past.'

'You persuaded Nick to leave the ship today.'

Hannah felt exasperated with the woman.

'No, I have done nothing of the sort.'

'So how come he's packing up now when he should be doing the next cruise with me and then taking his leave?'

Hannah struggled for control then shook her head slowly. 'I have no idea.'

Claudia's face was cracking up and she gave Hannah a look of defeat before turning and walking away leaving Hannah standing there.

Eventually Hannah reached the Vista

Lounge and sat looking out of the large picture windows forcing her mind to calm. It made no difference to her whether Nick stayed on the ship or flew home now. Once she was in her hotel in Barcelona, she wouldn't be in danger of bumping into either of them ever again.

What did worry her was the thought of leaving the friends she'd made onboard. Butterflies began to swirl in her stomach. Their friendship had supported her throughout the cruise but she wouldn't have that support in the hotel. She'd be all alone.

★   ★   ★

A coach was waiting on the quay to take those who were extending their stay to a hotel in the centre of Barcelona. Hannah recognised some of the couples she'd seen around the ship. They nodded and smiled at her then continued with their own conversations. She found a window seat near the back and was surprised at how calm she felt now she was away from both Nick and Claudia. Nick would be on his way to the airport and home to England and Claudia would be on the ship moodily getting ready for a new set of passengers. She leant back in her seat grateful that at last she would be left in peace to enjoy the rest of her holiday. Then she could go home and take up her old life again.

The hotel was huge, set back amid pleasant gardens, with wide marble steps leading into a bright and airy reception area graced with potted palms and beautiful floral arrangements. Hannah grabbed her luggage as soon as it was unloaded from the coach, checked in at reception, then went in search of her room.

It was light and spacious with a view over extensive lawns. Once she'd unpacked and tidied herself she went down to the grill for a late lunch, then took a walk round the grounds before retiring to her room for the rest of the afternoon. She really didn't have the energy for anything else. Tomorrow she'd explore the town.

★ ★ ★

She was up bright and early and down for breakfast before the restaurant was properly open. Having not eaten the previous night, she was starving and tucked into the cold buffet.

Half an hour later she skipped down the marble steps into the June sunshine and felt a warm glow of happiness lift her spirits. The hotel was near to a wide tree-lined boulevard that led all the way down to the harbour. Hannah hardly knew where to look, there was so much of interest all around her — artists and buskers and kiosks selling souvenirs. A detour down one of the narrow side streets led to the old part of the city with its beautiful Gaudi buildings. She lingered a while inside the magnificent cathedral, finding the air of tranquillity soothing. Muted golden light filtered through the beautiful stained glass windows and enhanced the slender Gothic columns that rose gracefully to support the vaulted roof.

Once out in the open air again she wandered through the narrow winding streets until she found herself on the waterside promenade with its parks and gardens. Eventually she reached the marina that Gary had told her was a pleasant place for a drink. She fancied a sit down after walking so far in the hot sun.

It was bustling with activity — yachts moving in and out of their moorings, people calling to one another, hosing decks, loading provisions, some just sitting idly with their hands round mugs of coffee, wrapped in thought. There were so many bars and restaurants she was spoilt for choice and eventually settled for one with tables in the shade and a good view of all the activity.

The sun was warm on her face as she sat with her coffee, the gentle clank of rigging against masts filling the air.

It was late afternoon before she got

back to the hotel, weary from all her exploring but happily content. But as soon as she shut the door to her room a sudden loneliness consumed her. Try as she might, she could not get Nick out of her mind. She'd felt so close to him on that last evening onboard. When he had taken her in his arms it had brought back so many memories and such strong feelings. His kiss had been so passionate yet he had offered nothing, just walked away. How could she have got it so wrong?

She dropped into the chair and covered her face with her hands. After long moments of utter despair she took her phone from her pocket and called Josie.

'Hi, Hannah, glad you remembered me!'

The minute she heard her sister's voice the pain in her heart began to fall away and warmth spread through her.

'Sorry. I've been so busy I haven't had time.'

'Did you see much of Nick?' Josie asked.

'Yes,' she managed in a small voice.

There was a silence the other end of the phone. Then Josie said, 'Come on, tell me what's happened.'

Hannah could hardly form the words her mouth was trembling so much. 'We did talk briefly.'

'You don't sound happy.'

'I'm not. I still feel the same about him. But what can I do?'

'Are you going to get together again?' Hannah could hear the caution in Josie's voice.

'No, he didn't even suggest it.'

'Phew, you had me worried there. I know how much he upset you last time.'

'He told me he doesn't want a permanent relationship with anyone, that his way of life doesn't allow for it. And I'll never see him again now I've left the ship.'

Again the pause. 'Hannah, once you're home with me and Charlie you'll soon settle down again and forget about him.'

'I don't think I will. But I have to try.'

'Good girl. Now you enjoy the rest of your holiday. You still have a week left. Make the best of it and don't let all this business with Nick spoil it. He let you down badly. He's not worth it.'

As Josie chattered on, Hannah began to regain some composure and told her about places she'd been, and about Nancy and Gary and how she'd made friends with Linda. Once she was back with Josie and could cuddle Charlie, Nick would fade into the background, just as Josie had said.

After putting the phone down she looked in the huge wardrobe and decided that if she made an effort to dress nicely and went down to the restaurant for dinner, it would make her feel a whole lot better.

The short navy dress with the pretty scooped neckline had always been a favourite. Gary had said how nice she looked in it when she'd worn it one evening on the ship. She took trouble with her make-up and was pleased that for once that her hair was behaving itself and curled neatly round her shoulders.

Going down in the lift, she smiled at the other guests and was rewarded with a few compliments. The dining room was very grand with waiters ushering people to their tables. They tried to find a small one and eventually settled her by an open window with a view of the gardens. She was comfortable there, out of the main part of the room. The menu was huge and, as she struggled to fathom what some of the dishes were, a shadow crossed the table.

Looking up, she saw Nick smiling down at her.

12

The shock of seeing Nick standing there rendered Hannah speechless.

He indicated the chair opposite.

'Would you mind if I join you?'

Once seated, he glanced at her uncertainly.

'What are you doing here?' she asked, when she finally found her voice.

'That wasn't the welcome I was hoping for.' He sighed, resignation settling on his features.

'I thought you'd be home by now,' she stuttered, not able to believe he was sitting there in front of her.

'I am,' he said, a ghost of a smile touching his lips. 'I live here in Barcelona. Have done for several years.'

She continued to stare at him in stunned disbelief. 'But how did you know where I was?'

'You told me you were doing the

extra week and I knew which hotel the company uses.'

Of course. All the clues had been there. She should have guessed what he was up to when he'd asked for leave from the ship.

The waiter came to take their order and Nick asked him to bring a bottle of white wine. He looked towards Hannah. 'I know that's what you drink. At least it used to be.'

'Yes, it still is,' she murmured, trying to recover from the shock.

The waiter disappeared and left them to further study the menu.

'Hannah, if you don't want me to stay I'll leave.'

'No, don't.' She was quick to respond, helplessly drawn by those smiling eyes.

The waiter came back with the wine and after pouring two glasses, stood waiting for their order.

Without looking at the menu Nick suggested the grilled salmon and she nodded. When the waiter had gone, he gave Hannah a tentative look.

'You told me you hated big menus, that you could never make up your mind.'

'You know I like salmon,' she mumbled, moved by this gesture.

He had only ever taken her out to dinner once, to a lovely little restaurant on the beach in Mykonos with decking overlooking the sea. They had fantasised about owning such a place and she had secretly dreamed that one day it might happen. After all these years he had remembered that small detail; how she had dithered over the menu and he had ordered for her.

Shaking herself back to the present, she brought her eyes to meet his again. 'But you didn't even look at the menu.'

His smile was relaxed. 'I know it off by heart. I help out here sometimes when I'm on leave.'

The waiter placed a bottle of wine on the table and he and Nick exchanged a few words.

It gave Hannah time to try to come to terms with this new situation. It was all so unexpected. She had convinced herself she would never see Nick again and then suddenly here he was, sitting in front of her.

When the waiter left he turned to her again, cleared his throat and straightened in his seat.

'After we talked last night I knew I had to see you again, so we could talk properly without Claudia causing trouble. That's why I asked for leave here.'

'What about Claudia?' she asked.

He let out a deep breath. 'I hope I never see her again. It depends if I go back on that ship. But she won't bother me in future. In the end I had to be firm and tell her I wasn't interested in any sort of relationship with her.'

'I bet that went down well,' she said bitterly.

He hunched his shoulders and looked away.

'What about you and Gary?' he said, bringing his focus back to her.

It took her by surprise. 'We're just friends. Why do you ask?'

'You seemed to be together a lot on

the ship and I saw you go ashore a few times. I thought maybe you two were getting pretty friendly.'

'Would it have mattered?'

He looked her in the eyes. 'Yes, it would.'

It silenced her.

'I didn't want us to get too close if you and Gary were getting together,' he explained.

'What do you mean by close?' she asked, feeling tension building.

'Hannah, do you think we could spend some time together this week?'

She wanted to say yes, but knew she shouldn't.

He'd made it quite clear last night on board that he didn't want any serious relationship with any woman. And he'd proved it with Claudia. It would just create more heartache and she'd had enough of that.

The waiter interrupted their conversation as he placed their meal in front of them. The salmon looked delicious but she had no appetite. Nick looked down at his plate, picked up his knife and fork then put it down again.

'The answer's no, isn't it? I'm sorry. I should have left well alone. I'll eat this, then go.'

Despite her best intentions she didn't want him to go. She didn't want him out of her life again. Would it really matter if they spent some time together? She couldn't feel worse than she did now. Should she take a little happiness while she could, and cope with the pain and hurt when she had to?

'I didn't say no,' she said quietly.

Nick brightened. 'You mean yes? I can show you all my favourite places. It's such a wonderful city.' He took her hand across the table. 'Hannah, we'll spend the whole day together tomorrow and I'll make sure it's one you'll never forget.'

She gave him a weak smile. That was exactly what she feared.

In spite of her fears, as they ate their food excitement began to bubble up inside her. Whatever lay ahead, she would have this one day with Nick.

That night she fell asleep in a warm glow of contentment, not letting a single worrying thought spoil her happiness. Whatever had gone wrong was in the past, Nick was here now. He wanted to be with her. And she wanted to be with him.

★　★　★

Just as Hannah was finishing breakfast Nick came striding into the hotel dining room as if he owned the place. He was dressed immaculately in well-fitting trousers and an open-necked shirt.

'You're up bright and early,' Hannah said as he joined her at the table.

A waiter came over immediately. 'Coffee?' he asked, looking from Nick to Hannah.

'That would be great, Joe,' Nick smiled.

'You two know each other?' Hannah asked as the waiter moved away.

'I know all the staff. I told you, I help out here.'

'How long have you been living here?'

'Couple of years now. It's a great city.'

'And I want to see all of it,' she said, full of expectation. 'Shall we get going?'

'Give a bloke time to drink his coffee,' Nick teased as the waiter placed a pot in front of him. 'We do have the whole day. I'll make sure you see everything, don't worry. It's a very compact city, so we can do it all on foot. I don't even own a car here.'

She waited impatiently for him to finish his coffee which he seemed to be taking his time over just to tease her. Typical of Nick; full of fun.

'I'll nip up to my room and get my things,' she said eventually, her heart singing as she anticipated the day ahead.

He nodded and she hurried towards the lift, smiling happily to herself.

Then caution kicked in. He'd only suggested they spend a day together. She mustn't read too much into it. But as she pulled a jacket from her wardrobe she decided to throw caution to the wind and enjoy this short time with Nick. It might only be one day but nothing was going to spoil it. Grabbing her handbag, she took the lift down to the foyer where he was chatting to one of the receptionists while he waited for her.

'We'll walk along Las Ramblas first. It's the main boulevard and runs in a straight line for over a mile right down to the port. It will give you a feel for the culture.'

Walking down the wide tree-lined boulevard with Nick by her side was different from yesterday. She hadn't told him she'd already walked the length of it. She didn't care where Nick took her so long as she was with him. Today she felt part of the lively scene, the tourists, the cafés and kiosks and, so it seemed to Hannah, a busker on every corner.

She stopped to watch an artist sketching a young boy while his parents looked on in amusement. When she turned, Nick had disappeared. She looked round in some dismay then spotted him walking towards her, a wide grin on his face and carrying a huge straw hat. He plonked it on top of her head.

'To keep the sun off your delicate skin.'

She posed and pulled a face at him and he gave a snort of laughter.

People were sitting in pavement cafés enjoying the warm June sunshine and socialising with friends. The vibrancy of the city was carrying her along and she could understand why Nick loved it so much.

A flurry of excitement consumed her when they finally reached the huge statue of Christopher Columbus.

'I've seen that great monument so many times from the deck of a ship. One of the passengers told me there was a lift inside that would take you right to the top,'

'Shall we do it?' Nick asked, with that mischievous look she remembered so well.

'We hardly had time to go ashore when we first met, did we?' she sighed.

'Just that one day in Mykonos.'

'When we found that little place on the beach.'

'The one we dreamed of owning one day.'

'When we thought dreams might come true.'

'Anything seemed possible.'

'Just a few weeks of happiness.' There was sadness in his eyes as they met hers. 'We were young. There was no way we could have done it.'

'I wish things could have worked out differently.'

Hannah shrugged. 'It's all in the past now.'

Nick squeezed her hand. 'Come on. No time for regrets. We'll go right to the top. I haven't done it yet so it's a first for both of us.'

The view from the top was spectacular. Hannah could see the cruise ships lined up along the quay and far out towards the ocean. She was staring across the city to the distant mountains when there was a tap on her shoulder and she turned to see Linda standing behind her.

'Hello, stranger!'

'I didn't know you were staying on for this extra week, too,' Hannah gasped.

'What a nice surprise for you.'

'But you weren't on the coach.'

'Not on the same one as you, I was on the second one,' Linda explained.

'Oh, I didn't realise there were two. But fancy meeting like this.'

'Not really that surprising,' Linda said. 'We've been told all week we have to go up the monument. So like all good tourists, here we are.'

Hannah felt a wonderful sense of relief. Linda would be at the hotel for the rest of the week. Her sensible down-to-earth attitude would sustain her if things got tough.

Nick looked on wondering who Linda was, so Hannah introduced them.

'You're not the Nick that Claudia was going on about in the salon, are you?' Linda said.

Nick shrugged awkwardly. 'Probably.'

'Well, I hope she doesn't catch up with you. I wouldn't like to be the one on the sharp end of her tongue!'

Nick shook his head. 'I doubt that will happen. She lives in England and I live here in Barcelona.'

'Sensible man. Anyway I might see you back in the hotel at some point, Hannah. I'm off to view the cathedral now.'

Once she'd gone Nick raised an eyebrow. 'Interesting lady.'

'She says what she thinks, but she's good company,' Hannah said.

'So you spent time together on the ship?'

'We went to the chateau in Sète. And we had breakfast together a couple of times. She's very anti-man.'

'More anti-Claudia, I'd have said.'

'Oh, Claudia wouldn't be her type.'

'Is Claudia anyone's type?'

'I thought she was yours.'

He shook his head slowly. 'Never. I just couldn't shake her off.'

'Well, you've managed it now. Is that why you asked for leave here? To escape from Claudia?'

His expression changed. 'No, I wanted to spend time with you, Hannah. It was the only way I could do it.'

So he wanted to be with her that much. So much that he had asked a favour of the company at short notice. She knew she mustn't get carried away. But they were here together and, at this moment, it was all that mattered.

'Come on. I'm going to take you to Café Maria for lunch,' he said, putting a hand to her back and guiding her towards the lift to go back down the monument. 'It's a little tapas bar run by Carlos and Maria. They serve the most delicious seafood. You'll love it.'

As they strode along the promenade Nick kept close, which Hannah was finding more and more difficult. It would have been so natural to slip her hand into his as the years began to fall away and they were together again.

When they turned off into the Old Quarter the streets became narrow with tall buildings giving shade from the heat of the sun. High above them balconies were decked with plants and flowers and occasionally a line of washing.

Finally he took her hand, as if he had read her thoughts, and when they had to step off the pavement to pass another couple on that narrow street he did not release it but gripped it even more tightly.

After walking through a maze of narrow winding back streets they reached a small square enclosed by tall buildings with colourful geraniums decking their balconies and music filtering through the shuttered windows, an oasis in the midst of the busy city.

A scatter of wooden tables stood in front of a doorway festooned with tumbling flowers, colourful parasols giving shade from the midday sun. Purple bougainvillea trailed down the side of a solid oak door. Each side of it were huge stone pillars supporting a crumbling archway.

A pretty young woman with thick, dark, slightly curly hair emerged as soon as she saw them and rushed to greet Nick.

There was lots of hugging and warm greetings in Spanish. Nick responded enthusiastically while Hannah stood smiling. Maria led them to a table with much fussing and almost immediately a bottle of wine appeared followed by a plate of prawns, some crusty bread and a bowl of olives, all amid much chatter and excitement.

Once Maria was happy they were settled, she busied herself with other customers.

Nick smiled at Hannah.

'They're a lovely couple. I eat here a lot when I'm home on leave. You'll meet Carlos eventually. He always comes out for a chat when he knows I'm here.'

Hannah sat back in the comfy cane chair. Above, palm trees wafting gently beneath a cloudless blue sky. A family sat at the next table, their little girl eyeing Hannah curiously, a mop of shiny black hair tied back in a huge blue ribbon.

Birdsong mingled with the burble of chatter and the odd burst of music. At one table an old man sat smoking and staring up at the sky. Another was reading a newspaper.

Hannah felt a warm glow of happiness lifting her spirits.

Carlos appeared with a plate of freshly grilled sardines, his handsome face and deep, dark eyes smiling a greeting.

Various other dishes followed . . . mussels cooked with garlic, crab's claws, Greek salad, thin slices of Parma ham.

When they had eaten their fill Nick leaned back in his seat.

'So tell me about your life. What are you doing now? I gather you gave up on the cruises.'

'That's right. I run a salon with my sister.'

'Still hairdressing then?'

'Always will be, I expect. But what about you? You seem to have got on well,' she said, desperate to turn the conversation away from herself for fear of inadvertently mentioning Charlie.

'True. I've moved up the ranks. But it's a strange life. You never know where they're going to send you next or how long you'll be away.'

'I thought that was what you liked. No ties. Freedom. Travel the world.'

'True — adventure was what I wanted.'

'And now?'

He shrugged. 'The life suits me. I couldn't work in a hotel. Whenever I help out there I'm always glad to get back on board for the next cruise.'

'No girlfriends in tow? Other than Claudia.'

'No girlfriends at all,' he said emphatically. Then he eyed her curiously. 'I know Gary isn't the one, but is there another?'

'No, I've had a few relationships but none of them worked out. I think I'm better on my own.'

'Me too. I'm staying with a mate here at the moment until I find somewhere to buy. He's letting me sleep in his spare room.'

So he didn't have a settled life, Hannah thought, then chided herself for building up unrealistic hopes.

★   ★   ★

Walking back along the promenade, they fell silent.

'I can see why you love this city,' Hannah said at last.

He turned to her and she thought she saw a glimpse of interest in his eyes, then quickly dismissed it. Nick had made it quite clear he was happy with the life he led. It was only asking for more hurt if she started imagining it could be different. His life was here in Barcelona and cruising the world. Hers was in England running a salon with her sister and caring for her son. They'd missed their chance.

It was late afternoon by the time they got back to the hotel.

'Can we meet for dinner later?' he

asked tentatively as they stood on the steps.

'That would be lovely,' she answered without a second thought.

'I'll come here for you at seven.'

'Could we go to Café Maria again? I loved it.'

'I was thinking that myself.' He leaned forward and brushed her lips softly, sending a shiver down her spine.

Alone in her hotel room, happiness bubbled up inside her but she cast aside any hopes for the future and instead concentrated on the evening ahead. The fluttering sensation lasted the whole time she was getting ready to meet him. She hadn't had this feeling for a long time and was determined to make the most of it.

When Nick walked through the doors of reception later he was dressed smartly in light trousers and shirt. Hannah thought how far he'd come from the young chef she had fallen in love with all those years ago. Before her stood a fine look-ing man, yet the gentle nature and spark of fun had not deserted him.

They were warmly welcomed by Carlos. He took their order from a menu chalked up on a board on the wall and was soon back with a dusty bottle of wine and two glasses.

Nick and he chatted for a while and Hannah was surprised at how fluent Nick had become in Spanish. Then Maria joined them and soon they were all hugging and laughing.

It was cooler in the square as evening drew on. Overhead lamps gave a warm glow. The tables were covered in a red checked cloths. A candle on each flickered gently, a bud vase with a single rose beside it.

When they were left alone Nick turned to Hannah. 'I'd love to own a place like this.'

'What, and give up cruising?'

'No, it's just a dream.'

'Do you ever wish . . . well, that we'd made our dream come true?' she said hesitantly, trying to suppress a bubble of hope rising inside her.

'You mean the beach bar in Mykonos? When we were young and foolish?'

The flurry of excitement she had felt was crushed instantly and they fell into silence, watching the movements around them, each with their thoughts and memories.

Eventually he turned his attention to her again. 'Hannah, I wish you weren't going home.'

She held his gaze. 'What else can I do?'

His eyes were studying her keenly. 'You could come here and live in Barcelona. Get a job hairdressing in one of the hotels.'

'And would you be here in this hotel?'

He bent his head and considered for a moment then looked up. 'No, I'd be away on the cruises some of the time.'

'Most of the time,' she stated, feeling a sudden rush of anger.

'I couldn't give it up, Hannah. I've worked too hard to get where I am, and I love my job.'

'So I would be changing my life and

moving from my home and a job I enjoy just to be here when you happened to come home on leave? It wouldn't matter that I might not like working in a hotel either?'

She'd only been testing him, hoping there might be some way they could be together with Charlie. But he hadn't changed. She had to accept it.

'Not the life you want,' he said with a sigh.

'No.' She turned away so he couldn't see the disappointment in her face.

'I suppose you're right. It was selfish of me to even suggest it.'

The arrival of the food broke into their conversation. Fillet of lemon sole with purple sprouting broccoli followed by a dark chocolate mousse. It looked delicious — and it was — but neither of them ate much.

Hannah pulled on her jacket as Nick got up to pay the bill. Nearly all the seats were taken now with people out for a pleasant evening. Carlos and Maria still made time to fuss over them as they left.

'Adios, amigo,' Carlos said, slapping Nick on the back.

Maria hugged Hannah. 'You come again soon,' she managed in English.

The sun was dipping low in the sky, casting soft shadows and bathing the magnificent buildings in a glorious golden light as they walked back to the hotel, yet Hannah could not dispel the feeling of gloom that had settled on her.

As they climbed the steps to the entrance Nick stopped and looked at her.

'It's been a lovely day. Thank you, Hannah.' His voice had dipped to a whisper.

Then he turned and walked back down to the street and, without a backward look, he disappeared from sight.

She watched him go, still unable to believe he had expected her to give up everything to fit in with his life without any consideration for hers. And when she had turned his idea down he had accepted it without any attempt at compromise.

She had been hoping for something

more; that at some point she would have felt able to tell him about Charlie, that he might be pleased he had a child. Yet she had known all along it was an unrealistic hope, as much of a dream as the beach bar in Mykonos.

Nick hadn't changed. Nothing and nobody would interfere with his way of life. She turned and went into the hotel with a sigh of resignation. Once back in her room, she phoned her sister.

'How are things with you and Nick?' Josie asked without preamble.

'He asked me to move to Barcelona, suggested I get a hairdressing job in one of the hotels.'

'But what about Charlie?'

'I didn't even mention him. There's no way I could bring Charlie here with Nick away all the time and me working in a hotel.'

'He might change his attitude if he knew he *had* a son.'

'He won't. He's too fond of his freedom. I'd be bringing Charlie away from a stable home where he's happy and loved. Then if things didn't work out and Nick upped and left us, he'd have his young life disrupted again. I couldn't put Charlie through that. He's fine with us.'

'Of course he is.'

Hannah couldn't help a sigh escaping her lips. 'I admit I was tempted.'

'So you *do* still want to be with him?'

'I don't know. I suppose deep down, yes. But Charlie has to come first.'

'You sound so sad.'

'It's hard,' she said, sighing.

'Oh, Hannah, I wish you were here and I could give you a hug.'

'I will be soon, Josie.'

She ended the call with a heavy heart then turned on the radio thinking some late night music would calm her. But the words of the song tore at her heart as tears rolled down her face . . . '*You're nobody till somebody loves you*'.

She'd had it on disc at home but could never listen to it after Nick had gone.

And now he was gone again.

13

As they were finishing breakfast together the next morning, Linda commented, 'So Nick's on leave in Barcelona, is he?'

'Yes.' Hannah knew this conversation would crop up and thought she was prepared for it. But after a restless night she wasn't at her best.

'Are you old friends?'

'We sailed on the same ship together once. A cruise of the Greek Islands.' She hoped that would satisfy Linda.

'So you met up for the day?'

'He lives here in Barcelona.'

'I did wonder why he was still here. Is this why Claudia was having a crisis?'

'I expect so . . . '

'I get the feeling there's more to this than you're letting on,' Linda said, giving her a quizzical look.

Hannah sighed. If Linda was going to be this persistent she might as well put her in the picture.

'Nick and I got very close on that cruise, but it only lasted three weeks, and it was five years ago now.'

'And you haven't been in touch since?'

Hannah bit her lip. 'No. I tried but he obviously went home and forgot all about me.'

'But you're still hankering after him?'

'I thought I'd got over him.'

'You obviously haven't.'

'Is it that obvious?' She was struggling to keep her voice steady.

'It's written all over your face, Hannah.' Hannah swallowed hard to try to gain control. 'Is he keen to start the relationship up again?' Linda asked.

'He suggested that I come and live here in Barcelona and work in a hotel salon.'

'Will you do that?'

'How do I know he wouldn't go off with someone else eventually and leave me? He's evidently had lots of girlfriends but none of them have lasted long.'

Linda emptied the coffee pot into her

cup. 'And how do you know this?'

'Gary told me. I'd just be filling the gap until another one came along,' Hannah said bitterly.

Linda eyed Hannah over the rim of her cup as she sipped her coffee then put her cup down.

'In that case you can't let your emotions for this man take over. He's let you down once already after all. They all do in the end. You have to be strong, Hannah.'

'I know, but it's hard.' She could feel a lump forming in her throat.

'Not as hard as being let down again. If he really wanted your relationship to work he'd be trying a bit harder,' Linda said, firmly.

Hannah nodded without looking at her.

Linda saw her struggle.

'Look, I'm here for you. We can stick together all week and not give him a chance.'

'Thanks, Linda, I think I'd like that, if that's all right with you,' she murmured.

'Come on then. Let's get off before

he comes looking for you again!'

Hannah felt some relief in having opened her heart to Linda and the prospect of a day together. She certainly didn't fancy spending it alone.

Then a thought struck her. 'But what about Ralph? Is he here in the hotel?'

'No, he went home straight from the cruise. We have no men to worry about. Now cheer up and let's get on our way. Barcelona, here we come!'

Hannah felt a smile coming on.

'Let's go,' she said, getting up from the table.

★ ★ ★

First they visited an art gallery that Linda had on her list of things to do. She stood in front of a strange painting, a frown on her face. It was an abstract design with lots of overlapping squares with thick brush strokes of paint.

'Never could understand that sort of art,' she said dismissively 'Let's move on.'

They did a couple more galleries and

emerged into a big open square just on lunchtime.

'Don't know about you but I'm not terribly hungry,' Linda said.

'Nor me, but I could murder a cup of coffee. That place over there looks inviting.'

Hannah pointed across the square to where brightly coloured awnings gave shade from the blazing sun.

'It certainly seems popular. Let's see if we can get a table.'

A waiter found one for them, nicely positioned so they could absorb the atmosphere as they watched people strolling by.

Once seated and having ordered their coffee Linda turned to Hannah.

'Are you sure you wouldn't like to live here? Even if it was only for a few years. Get away from the dreary weather at home? There must be plenty of jobs for hairdressers, I'd have thought. If it didn't work out you could always go home again. I suppose it would give you a chance to see if Nick really is serious.'

If only it were that simple, Hannah thought.

'No, it would just be a casual arrangement. Someone to come home to when he's on leave. Until he gets bored and finds someone else.'

'Did he say that?'

'Of course not.'

'So what makes you so sure of it?'

'I know what he's like. Love them and leave them seems to be his motto.'

'Maybe that's because he's never found the right person. Perhaps he never got over you.'

Hannah felt a moment of disquiet, then instantly dismissed it.

'If he'd cared enough he wouldn't have given up so easily.'

Linda shrugged. 'Fair enough. So what's next on our list?' she said, getting out the guide book.

It had been difficult keeping Charlie out of the conversation but Hannah really did not want any more advice. She knew what was best for her son and it wasn't here in Barcelona with her working in a hotel and Nick away on cruises. He was safe and happy in Leicester, and that was where he was staying. She had no intention of disrupting his young life.

After the Picasso museum they spent the rest of the afternoon admiring the Art Nouveau architecture of the beautiful buildings around the old town. Linda was very knowledgeable and made the whole experience more interesting.

Then they walked back to the hotel in the mellow light of early evening. Both agreed it had been a good day and decided to go back to their rooms to shower and change then meet up again in the bar.

As soon as Hannah opened her door she saw the folded piece of paper lying on the floor and knew it was from Nick. She opened it apprehensively. He wanted to know where she'd been all day!

She screwed it tightly in a ball and threw it in the waste paper basket. So he had expected her to wait around all day in case he showed his face? He hadn't even made any arrangement. How typical of Nick! Expecting her to be there when it suited him. How many times had she waited in vain? Waited for emails that didn't arrive. Waited for phone calls that didn't happen. Well, she'd done enough waiting!

She wasn't going to respond to this note. She didn't want to see him ever again. She'd had a lovely carefree day with Linda, much better than the heartache that always accompanied time with Nick.

Rage bubbled inside her all the while as she showered and dressed. It was only in the lift on her way to meet Linda that she calmed down.

'Do you mind if we eat out tonight?' She told Linda about the note as they ordered their drinks at the hotel bar. 'I have a feeling he might turn up, and I do not want to see him.'

'OK, so a little subterfuge is called for.'

Hannah gave a hoot of laughter and felt herself relax into the mood of the evening.

They found a small restaurant down one of the back streets of the town where Linda was confident Nick wouldn't find them. The food was good, the ambience lively with locals occupying most of the tables. During the evening a couple of musicians played guitars and sang. They drank a lot of wine and didn't mention men at all.

'Tomorrow we could visit the maritime museum. We get to see a full sized replica of a galleon. Out in the courtyard there's a café and included in the price is a visit to the Santa Eulalia tall ship.'

Hannah snorted. 'You've been at that guide book again.'

'Sure have. We don't want to waste time aimlessly wandering, do we?'

'Definitely not.'

Hannah didn't really care where they went so long as she didn't encounter Nick.

★ ★ ★

Each morning dawned bright and warm with new adventures planned. They managed to avoid Nick and, even though he left messages for her every day, each one becoming more fraught, Hannah didn't responded to any of them.

It was the last evening before she was to leave the hotel for home. After closing her case Hannah sat on the bed staring into space for some minutes, then she phoned Josie to arrange a pick-up at the airport the next day.

'Oh, Hannah, I was just about to phone you.'

Hannah could hear the panic in Josie's voice. 'What's wrong?'

'Everything! I've sprained my wrist and had to cancel appointments. And play school sent Charlie home with a temperature. Some bug that's going round. Clive wants half the business as part of the divorce settlement. I don't know how I'm going to raise the money to pay him off. I've got invoices mounting up and one of our suppliers has gone bust. I'm so stressed!'

'Josie, stop. Is Charlie OK?'

'Don't you worry about him. He'll be right as rain by the time you get home tomorrow. You know what kids are like, always picking up something.'

'Is your wrist badly injured?'

'No, but it's strapped up and I can't do anything with it. Fortunately I managed to get Kelly to come in. She's been great.'

'And I'll be home tomorrow. So just hang on and stop worrying.'

'But what can we do about Clive? I don't want him interfering in our business.'

'We'll pay him off.'

'But how? The business is doing well but we don't have that sort of money.'

'We'll re-mortgage, or get a loan.'

'Oh, I'll be so glad to have you back. I don't know what I'd do without you with all this going on. But what about you and Nick?'

'Nothing to worry about there.'

How could she even consider a life in Spain with all this going on at home and Charlie to consider?

'You're not going to move to Barce-lona, are you?' There was panic in Josie's voice.

'Of course not,' she said.

'Hannah, are you sure you don't want to live there and be with him?'

'No,' Hannah said in a determined voice.

'But I don't want you coming home for me. I know I threw a wobbly just then but I want you to do what's best for you and Charlie. Have you told him about Charlie?'

'No.'

'So, he still doesn't know he has a son?'

'No. Josie, what would be the point? He wouldn't want the commitment of a child. I don't want him involved. It would only complicate matters.'

'I suppose it would.'

'I'll be on the plane tomorrow,' she said.

'Oh, it will be so good to have you home. I'm getting into such a tizzy over all this. I'm really not cut out for this business.'

'Josie, please stop worrying about it.'

'Yes, yes, I already have. I'll be at the airport to meet you and I've planned a special meal for us.'

Hannah put her phone down with a heavy heart.

★   ★   ★

It was while she was getting ready to meet Linda for dinner that Nick appeared at her door. She took a deep breath and let him in. He stood awkwardly in front of her, tall and straight, and her heart began thumping.

'Hannah, will you have dinner with me tonight? There's something I need to talk to you about.'

He stepped towards her and put out his hands but she moved back to avoid contact.

'No, I don't think that's a good idea.'

'It's important, Hannah,' he said intently.

'No. I'm having dinner with Linda.'

'But you go home tomorrow.'

'Yes, and I still have packing to do.'

'That's why I need to talk to you now.'

She made herself look straight at him.

'Well, say what you have to say and then go. I'm meeting Linda in half an hour.'

He let a brief pause fall and ran a hand over his hair. 'I can't discuss it with you here while you're standing glaring at me.'

'Then go. Whatever it is will make no difference. You've left it all too late.'

There was a short tense silence. 'Hannah, please. This may make you change your mind.'

She remained tight-lipped and silent as she stood aside and indicated he should leave. He gave her a look of defeat and she held his gaze as he hesitated a moment. Then he continued out into the corridor.

She quietly closed the door and stood

riveted to the spot. Then she picked up her phone and called Linda in her room.

'Linda, I can't make it this evening.'

'He's found you and talked you into getting back with him, right?' Linda's tone startled her.

'No, he just wanted me to have dinner with him; said there was something he needed to talk to me about.'

'And you won't listen.'

'Linda, we've spent time together over the past two weeks and nothing has changed. All he's suggested is that I move to Barcelona and get a job in a hotel while he carries on with his life. Why do I have to listen to any more of it?'

'Hannah, he's been here every day looking for you. He hasn't given up even though you've not answered one of his notes. You haven't picked up his calls. I've seen the look on your face when you've told me it was a wrong number. A bloke doesn't behave like that if he's not keen. Surely you can hear him out?'

There was a silence. The phone went dead and she knew Linda was on her way over. There was a tap at the door and Linda walked in.

'Right, get your gear on, patch your face up, and get yourself down to that foyer. You are going to have dinner with that man tonight,' Linda announced before she had even closed the door.

Hannah looked up in alarm. 'No, I am not! You've been telling me all week to ignore him. Why this sudden change of mind?'

Linda plonked herself on the bed beside Hannah. 'I've just spent twenty minutes with the bloke. He's down there in the bar and he's desperate to talk to you.' When she saw the look on Hannah's face her expression softened. 'There's something he wants to discuss with you. And you need to hear it.'

'No, Linda, I do not want to hear it. I've made up my mind to cut him right out of my life. All he ever does is hurt me.'

'Maybe, but I honestly believe you

should listen to what he has to tell you. So get a move on.' Linda gave her a stern look and left.

Hannah stared at the door as it closed then dropped her head into her hands, hopelessly confused. She wanted with all her heart to spend this last evening with Nick. And he was waiting for her in this hotel.

Tomorrow she would be home with Josie and Charlie, well out of his reach. If he had something worthwhile to say to her then she would listen.

After showering she wound her hair into a coil at the back of her head and slipped into a simple linen dress she always felt comfortable in. If she was to spend this evening with Nick, she wanted his lasting memory of her to be a good one.

Inside her jewellery pouch lay a tiny heart-shaped locket on a silver chain. She hadn't worn it for years but always had it close to her. Just knowing it was there gave her comfort. She carefully lifted it out, opened the clasp that held the two halves of the heart together and gazed at the tiny photos inside. Her heart swelled with love and pain.

Nick had given it to her on their last evening together on that first cruise. They were out on deck standing by the ship's rail in the moonlight. Above, the sky was littered with stars, the deep, dark sea beneath them stirred only by the motion of the ship as it took them ever closer to their final port. He'd looked shy and uncertain as he drew the small package from his pocket. When she'd opened the box her legs had gone wobbly and she'd had to hold back the tears.

'I've put a photo of me inside but I didn't have one of you. You must put one in and then we will always be together,' he'd told her.

And there they still were. Nick and Hannah, facing each other inside the locket. But it had all been romantic nonsense. They were far too young to make those sorts of promises.

But the memory had never faded.

★ ★ ★

Nick was waiting for her in reception. He looked tired and drawn and yet more handsome than ever. As she approached, his lips moved in a tentative smile. Without speaking, he rested an arm lightly on her back to guide her into the restaurant.

He'd arranged for them to have a table in a corner of the room. As soon as they were seated a waiter was at their side. Nick ordered for both of them and the waiter gave him a knowing smile. He was obviously one of Nick's friends and would ensure they were not disturbed during their meal.

All around them was chatter and laughter, yet Hannah was aware only of Nick sitting opposite to her. Conversation was going to be difficult and she hoped the ordeal would soon be over. Their final parting would be heart-wrenching and she knew it would have been better if they had not met tonight. Yet she had to hear what he was so desperate to tell her.

A bottle of champagne arrived in a bucket of ice. Nick popped the cork and began to pour into the elegant flutes. Hannah watched as bubbles rose through the amber liquid. He handed one to her with an unsteady hand and she noticed her own hand was shaking, so she quickly placed the glass on the table.

She watched as he played around with the food on his plate. What could be so important that he was making such a fuss about telling her? She wasn't going to quiz him about it. He'd tell her in his own good time. Though she was curious to hear what he would say she felt remarkably calm knowing her mind was now firmly set and his words would have no influence over her.

The roast duck looked appetising. She picked at the meal and sipped the champagne but it didn't produce the bubbly feeling it usually did.

Nick kept glancing at her. He'd

noticed the locket and remembered. They didn't say a word but both knew the significance of that little heart and were experiencing the same emotions.

Suddenly he placed his cutlery back down on the table and stood up abruptly.

'Can we go outside? I can't talk to you properly in here with so many people and all the noise.'

She nodded and got up.

The atmosphere had become claustrophobic and she was only too happy to escape into the fresh air. Nick spoke to the waiter and then guided her towards the large glass doors that led onto the terrace. He tried to take her hand as they walked through the beautiful grounds but she edged away. At the end of a tree-lined path they emerged into a clearing with a wooden table at its centre. Nick pulled a chair for her to sit and then took the other one himself so they faced each other. The moon cast an eerie blue light through the dark trees and though it was warm, she felt herself shiver and pulled the wrap she'd been carrying closer round her shoulders.

'So what's all this about?' she asked as he sat watching her intently.

He hesitated a moment, seemed nervous, disconcerted. Finally he cleared his throat and spoke. 'Hannah, I don't want us to be parted ever again.'

'I've told you, Nick. I won't move to Barcelona.'

'I know. I understand. You don't want to work in a hotel. And you're not happy with me being away so much. It was selfish of me to suggest it.' He hesitated. 'I have another idea.'

She eyed him suspiciously. 'What now?'

'When we talked about that little beach bar in Mykonos . . . '

Her heart began to beat wildly. 'Yes?'

'I only found out last night . . . '

His face became more animated.

'Found out what?'

'Carlos is selling Café Maria. Maria's expecting a baby and they want to move back to be near their family.'

'And you want to buy it?' she said, trying to keep her voice steady.

He took a deep breath. 'I want *us* to buy it.'

'Us?' she blinked in bewilderment.

His face was alight.

'You loved the place, didn't you? As soon as Carlos told me, I knew it was the answer. We could run it together, you and me. Make our dream come true.'

A thrilling current moved through her as he held her gaze. He was offering her everything she had dreamed of.

'There are rooms above where we could live,' he was telling her as a voice of caution crept into her mind. *He doesn't know about Charlie.*

'It would make a lovely home for us. Carlos showed me,' Nick continued with enthusiasm.

Her stomach began to churn. Would he want a child in that home? She'd have to bring Charlie here, bring him to a strange country. Nick still didn't know he had a child. How would he react when he did?

'You'd have to give up your job on the cruise ships,' she said, playing for time.

'I would. But running Café Maria with you would be worth it,' he said, looking deep into her eyes.

Another thought intruded. Could she run Café Maria with Nick and still look after Charlie?

'I'd be leaving Josie on her own in the salon.' She was thinking aloud now.

His smile was reassuring. 'She'd get another hairdresser to take your place.'

Yes, Kelly would gladly step in, she knew that. But how would Josie feel if she took Charlie away? And what if Nick got bored, found someone else, left her? It had happened before. And would he be so keen on this idea when he knew she had a child to support? It all seemed so impossible.

'Nick, there's something I need to tell you,' she blurted out.

He stopped talking and gave her his full attention. With her mind in a turmoil of doubt and indecision, her phone rang. She tensed. It could only be Josie. After only a short exchange she ended the call and stood up.

'Hannah, what's wrong?'

He was instantly beside her, concern etched on his face.

'Nick, I have to get home. It's Charlie. He's been taken into hospital!' She could feel the blood drain from her face and she began to shake all over. 'I have to go now. They suspect meningitis.'

Nick took her arm to steady her. 'Let's get back into the hotel.'

He continued to hold on to her as they walked down the path. She didn't pull away this time, needing the comfort and reassurance it gave her.

'It's too late to go this evening. All the flights will be booked,' he told her.

'I have to try,' she said in a shaky voice.

The more he tried to calm her the more hysterical she became. Eventually he sat her in one of the chairs in reception.

'I'll try and get one for you if it's that important,' he said, insisting she stay put.

Hannah watched as he walked over to reception, grateful he was taking over. He spoke to the woman behind the desk. The woman picked up the phone. They talked and there appeared to be several phone calls. Then Nick came back to her.

'They've managed to find a flight. We have to go straight away. Are you packed?'

'Yes,' she said jumping up from her seat.

'Can you make it to your room on your own?'

She gave him a tight smile and nodded.

'How do I get to the airport?' she said, as panic rose again.

She had never felt so totally alone and scared as she stood in that hotel knowing she had to get home through the night to her sick child.

He moved towards her, took her in

his arms and held her trembling body until she calmed. It was all she needed and she clung to him as if she would never let him go. Then he took her hands firmly in his and gave her a reassuring smile.

'The porter will come with you and bring your luggage down while I get the car.'

'You don't have a car.'

'I've borrowed one.'

'What, you'll take me to the airport?'

'Yes, now get a move on. We haven't got long,' he said gently but firmly.

Suddenly she found an inner strength. With Nick beside her she could do it.

When she got back to her room Linda was waiting outside.

'Come on, girl, you have to get moving. Don't want to miss that flight.'

'You know about Charlie?'

'Nick phoned me. Told me your nephew was ill and you needed to get home. He asked me to make sure you were OK while he's gone to get the car.'

Hannah perched on the edge of the

bed shivering while Linda rounded up her belongings. Her legs were so shaky she felt sure they wouldn't support her much longer.

'Now, don't start panicking. It's probably a false alarm. Happens all the time with young children. He'll be back to normal by the time you get home.'

Hannah listened but wasn't comforted. All she could think about was getting to Charlie.

'Right, get yourself down to reception. Nick should be back by now.'

Linda gave her luggage to the waiting porter then took Hannah's arm and led her towards the lift. As they waited for it to arrive she looked at Hannah and tilted her head to one side.

'Is this Josie's child?'

Hannah shook her head.

'He's yours, isn't he?'

Hannah nodded.

'And you don't think Nick would want to take on another man's child, is that why you keep turning him away?'

Hannah shook her head. 'He's not

another man's child.'

'What? He's Nick's?'

'Yes.' She nodded miserably.

'And he doesn't know?'

'I haven't told him.'

'Are you going to?'

'No, it's best now if he thinks he's Josie's.'

'Best for who?'

'I was going to tell him.' She tried to explain but the words refused to form on her lips.

'I think you ought to.'

The lift arrived and, as there were others in it, there was no possibility of continuing the conversation.

Nick was waiting. Hannah said a tearful goodbye to Linda and as they hugged Linda whispered in her ear. 'Tell him, Hannah.'

As they drove through the night to the airport Hannah began to calm and her breathing steadied.

There was a queue for the terminal carpark and Nick turned and glanced at her.

She managed a weak smile. 'Will you come with me into the terminal?' she asked, still feeling she wanted his support.

'I'll do better than that,' he said, giving her a fond glance. 'I've booked seats for both of us.'

'You're coming with me?'

Relief flowed through her as she realised she would not be facing this alone.

'I couldn't let you travel on your own, the state you're in. Now stop worrying. You'll be home in a few hours.' He paused as if considering. 'By the way, who is Charlie? I assumed he was Josie's. But I have a feeling he's more than a nephew.'

Linda's words came to her.

'He's my son,' she said in a very small voice. There was a minute shift of expression as Nick registered what she was telling him then he turned back to the wheel as the traffic began to move. She could see it had unnerved him but he recovered quickly, parked the car and got her luggage out of the boot.

Quietly she followed him into the terminal.

It was only when he had her seated in the café with a cup of coffee in front of her that he finally spoke again.

'How old is Charlie?'

His voice was so quiet it was almost impossible to make out the words.

She felt unable to deceive him any longer.

'He's four years and three months.'

She hardly dared breathe while she waited for him to speak.

He nodded slowly. 'My child . . . '

He sat studying her keenly until she could stand it no longer and turned away so that he could not see the anguish in her face.

They fell silent.

When she eventually raised her head he was looking at her, his face inscrutable.

'And you let me believe he was Josie's son,' he said quietly and calmly. 'Why did you do that? Was it because you didn't want me in his life?'

'I didn't think you'd want to be,' she responded without looking at him.

There was a long silence as he struggled with his emotions. Then he got up and walked over to the departure board.

She watched as he wandered off among the duty free, stopping to pause occasionally although she knew he wasn't interested in the products. Eventually he disappeared from view.

She sat rigid, desperately praying that he would eventually come back. It seemed a lifetime before he did and she had no idea what to expect as he seated himself opposite her at the table, his expression unfathomable.

She stared mutely at her hands resting on the table, waiting for him to speak.

A moment later he reached over and lifted her chin. He wasn't frowning now. A hint of a smile touched his lips.

'Phone your sister and check on Charlie,' he said gently.

14

Hannah moved away from Nick. He sensed she needed some privacy to talk to Josie so turned and stared out through the windows at planes taking off and landing, deep in thought.

After only a few moments Hannah put the phone back in her pocket. As she moved to the table Nick got to his feet and walked towards her.

'He's going to be OK,' she told him, feeling weak with relief. 'His temperature's coming down. They've done tests. Evidently it's some virus he's picked up. Nothing more serious.'

She could see he was visibly moved.

'You don't have to come with me now,' she said, smiling sadly up at him.

'Don't you want me to?' he said in alarm.

'Yes, of course I do. I just thought . . .' she stammered, not knowing what to say.

'Then I'm coming.' He bent his head and considered for a moment. 'Hannah, is Charlie the reason you were so hesitant about taking over Café Maria with me?'

She nodded miserably.

'You don't want to bring Charlie to Barcelona? You don't think I'd be a good father to him? Is that it?'

'I didn't think you'd want the responsibility of a child.'

'Hannah, how could you think that?'

She was silent.

'I want to come home with you and meet my son,' he said, quietly but firmly.

She was so overcome with emotion she could hardly speak.

'I want us to be together. You, me and Charlie,' he continued.

'It's what I want too,' she said, hardly able to form the words. 'But I'll have to take Charlie away from Josie and she's looked after him all his life when I couldn't. It will break her heart.'

He closed his eyes and was thoughtful.

'Then I'll move back to England.'

His words hung in the air as she stared at him, unable to believe what he was telling her.

'I'll find a job in a hotel.'

'But you wanted to take over Café Maria!' she exclaimed.

'Not without you.'

'But you said you couldn't work in a hotel.'

'I'll do whatever it takes.' His voice was firm with resolve.

'You mean you'd give up the cruises and work in a hotel in Leicester?' she asked incredulously.

'Yes.'

'But you love Barcelona.'

'Not without you there.'

'You'll do all that for me?' she gasped.

'I would do anything for you, Hannah.'

Happiness was overflowing and her heart was thumping so hard she could hardly contain it.

Although charged with emotion, his voice came out strong and steady.

'It stopped me from being with you

once. It won't stop me again.'

'But you told me on the ship that — '

'That was before,' he interrupted.

'Before what?'

He moved towards her and took her hands in his. 'Before I realised how much I wanted you by my side. No amount of adventure could make up for losing you again.' The catch in his voice told her how emotional he was. 'I love you, Hannah, and I promise I will never let you down again.'

'Nick, I can't let you do this,' she breathed.

'You mean you don't want us to be together?'

'Of course I do! More than anything in the world,' she cried.

'Do you believe me when I say that this time it's forever?' His voice was low and expressive.

She nodded, unable to utter a word. How could she not believe him now when he was prepared to give up so much to be with her?

'So what's stopping us now?' He smiled.

'Nothing,' she managed to murmur through trembling lips.

'What is it?' he asked gently when he saw a shadow cross her face.

'I wish it could have been Café Maria,' she whispered through her tears.

He pulled her close and silenced her with a lingeriing kiss.

'So long as we have each other that's all that matters,' he said softly.

Her phone rang and she fumbled for it, hoping it wasn't bad news. With her heart in her mouth she answered.

'Josie, what's wrong? Is it Charlie?'

'No, no, he's improving by the minute. In fact he'll be home again tomorrow. I just had this wonderful idea. It was when we were talking just then. Why don't I come and live in Spain, too?'

There was a pause while she waited for a reply that never came, for Hannah was too choked with emotion. Eagerly, Josie went on, 'You do want to stay in Barcelona with Nick, don't you?'

A feeling of pure joy spread through Hannah and at last she cried, 'Yes!

What a wonderful idea, Josie!'

'Phew, you had me worried then. I thought for a minute I'd misread the signs.'

'Oh, Josie, you know me so well,' she managed through tears of joy.

'I could tell you were worried about leaving me, but this way I can sell the salon and pay Clive off,' Josie rattled on in excitement. 'You know how unhappy I've been since Clive left me and I need a change.'

'Oh, Hannah, it would be so lovely to wake up to sunshine in the morning and feel warm! No more worry about bills and invoices. I could find a little flat and get a hairdressing job in one of those big hotels you talked about. There'd be lots of people and I'd never be lonely . . . and Charlie will be where he belongs, Hannah.'

Hannah ended the call with a huge grin on her face. She stood savouring the moment, her heart full of joyful anticipation, before she turned to Nick, took a deep breath — and it all came tumbling out in a rush.

His eyes widened and he actually laughed for joy. 'You mean we *can* live in Barcelona?'

'Yes!' she squealed, as happiness threatened to overflow. 'And take over Café Maria. And make our dream come true.'

'You, me and Charlie,' he whispered.

'But who'll look after him while we run the café? Josie will be working,' she said in alarm as the thought struck her.

'We both will. And all the customers will make such a fuss over him. I know most of them already. He'll love it!'

Of course. Café Maria was the sort of place where a child could grow up in safety.

Nick's face creased into a broad smile as he picked her up and swung her round and round. Then he put her down and kissed her gently on the lips and she let that kiss banish all doubts and anguish from her mind.

Charlie was safe. And Nick was by her side.

As he pulled her closer in that

crowded airport, nothing mattered but being in the arms of the man she loved.

Her future now held a promise. The promise of love fulfilled.

We do hope that you have enjoyed reading this large print book.

Did you know that all of our titles are available for purchase?

We publish a wide range of high quality large print books including:
Romances, Mysteries, Classics
General Fiction
Non Fiction and Westerns

Special interest titles available in large print are:
The Little Oxford Dictionary
Music Book, Song Book
Hymn Book, Service Book

Also available from us courtesy of Oxford University Press:
Young Readers' Dictionary
(large print edition)
Young Readers' Thesaurus
(large print edition)

For further information or a free brochure, please contact us at:
Ulverscroft Large Print Books Ltd.,
The Green, Bradgate Road, Anstey,
Leicester, LE7 7FU, England.
Tel: (00 44) **0116 236 4325**
Fax: (00 44) **0116 234 0205**

Other titles in the
Linford Romance Library:

A YEAR IN JAPAN

Patricia Keyson

When ex-librarian Emma announces she's accepted a year-long position to teach English in Japan, the news shocks her grown children. Enjoying single life after half a year of estrangement from her husband Neil, Emma can't wait to embark upon her adventure in three weeks. Then Neil is hospitalised after a car accident, and needs a carer at home while he recovers. Emma is the only one available to help. Three weeks — can Neil make up for lost time before Emma leaves, and will she let him back into her heart?